THE NIGHTMARE MACHINE

Bugged out . . .

Zak heard the skitter of tiny feet. *Thousands* of tiny feet. They scraped along the ground all around him. Something brushed across his foot. Then again, and again.

Scratch, scratch, scratch!

Something crawled up his pant leg. Panicked, Zak tried to brush it away, and felt something soft and hairy and many-legged cling to the back of his hand. Then it started to crawl up his arm.

More of the skittering creatures were crawling up his pant legs. He felt them crawling inside his pant legs and inside his shirtsleeves, pushing their way up his shirt, crawling out from under his collar and scrambling around the back of his neck. Zak wildly thrashed his arms and legs about, trying to get the horrible creatures off him.

He felt something tugging and biting at his hair. Zak opened his mouth to scream, and a dozen hairy legs scrambled past his lips.

Look for a preview of Star Wars: Galaxy of Fear #5, *Ghost of the Jedi,* in the back of this book!

STAR WARS®
GALAXY of FEAR

BOOK 4

THE NIGHTMARE MACHINE

JOHN WHITMAN

BANTAM BOOKS
NEW YORK · TORONTO · LONDON · SYDNEY · AUCKLAND

For my parents, who helped me dream.

THE NIGHTMARE MACHINE
A BANTAM BOOK : 0 553 506552

First publication in Great Britain

PRINTING HISTORY
Bantam edition published 1997

Bantam Books are published by Transworld Publishers Ltd,
61–63 Uxbridge Road, London W5 5SA,
in Australia by Transworld Publishers (Australia) Pty Ltd,
15–25 Helles Avenue, Moorebank, NSW 2170,
and in New Zealand by Transworld Publishers (NZ) Ltd,
3 William Pickering Drive, Albany, Auckland.

Printed and bound in Great Britain by
Cox & Wyman Ltd, Reading, Berkshire

PROLOGUE

The scientist stormed into his laboratory, overturning tables and smashing vials of smoking liquid to the floor as he passed. His servants—both droids and living creatures—scattered to avoid his anger. The scientist reached the center of his giant fortress and sat down before five computer screens.

"Give me a progress report on Project Starscream," the scientist commanded.

One by one, the five screens came to life.

Three of them showed nothing but static.

Project Starscream was a top-secret program that the scientist had developed for the Emperor. There were six steps. Three of them had already taken place. The fourth and fifth were ready to go. The sixth and final stage was set to take place in the scientist's citadel itself.

The scientist had worked hard to keep his plans secret. Only a few people in the entire galaxy had known of Project Starscream's existence. No one suspected that the scientist was hatching a plot to bring the entire universe to its knees.

Until now.

Of the five experiments, three had already been ruined. The scientist glared at the blank screens.

D'vouran, the living planet. The zombies of Necropolis. And just a few days before, the plague virus on Gobindi. One by one, three of his experiments had been destroyed. Not by Rebel commandos, but by the most unlikely of enemies: two kids and a droid, led by a meddling anthropologist.

The scientist whispered his enemy's name like a curse. "Hoole."

Somehow Hoole and the brats he watched over had learned of Project Starscream. Although they didn't know everything yet, they knew enough to be dangerous. But they would not live long enough to learn the final secret. The scientist planned to make them pay for interfering with his experiments.

He looked up at the fourth view screen and smiled. Stage Four was ready for testing. And he knew just who to test it on. . . .

CHAPTER 1

"Don't make any sudden moves!" Zak hissed. Beside him, his sister, Tash, obeyed, and the two Arrandas froze.

Before them, a remote sentry droid hovered. It didn't look dangerous—it was only a tiny metal ball covered with small silver studs. But Zak, who tried to keep up with the latest technology, knew that it was a Balmorran HK-130 sentry droid. Each of those little silver studs could fire a stun beam strong enough to put a bantha to sleep.

It was early morning, and Zak and Tash were inside the headquarters of the Galactic Research Academy on the planet Koaan. Their uncle, Hoole, an anthropologist, kept an office at the Academy, although he rarely visited there. He spent most of his time traveling across the galaxy, studying alien cultures as part of his research. Zak and Tash had gone with him on several of these field trips. Lately, however, those trips had turned deadly. After their last adventure on the planet Gobindi—where Tash had nearly been killed by a deadly virus—Hoole had taken them directly to the Galactic Research Academy.

"I've got a bad feeling about this," Tash whispered as the sentry droid continued to study them.

"Relax," Zak whispered.

"How can I relax with that thing scanning me?" his sister grumbled. "What if it fires at us?"

Zak held back a sigh of irritation. For someone who read all day, Tash didn't know much about technology.

"This is a trouble-seeker droid," he explained, trying to stay as calm as possible. "The Academy custodians probably let them loose overnight to watch for maintenance trouble or vandals. This one's just trying to decide if we're a threat or not. Once it makes up its mind, it will let us go."

"Or shoot us," Tash whispered. "Who's to say it's not going to—"

Before she could finish her sentence, the hovering

ball of firepower turned and zipped away. Zak grinned. "See, technology can be your friend if you let it."

"Let's just get on with this," Tash replied.

Soon after they had arrived at the Research Academy, Uncle Hoole had vanished without a word, leaving Zak and Tash with a thousand unanswered questions.

They had decided to find the answers on their own.

They had located one of the Research Academy's core computer libraries. These weren't exactly maximum security zones, but Zak and Tash knew they weren't supposed to be there without supervision.

They were going to sneak a look at Uncle Hoole's computer files.

The two Arranda children had been adopted by Hoole seven months ago when their parents and everyone they knew had been killed during the destruction of the planet Alderaan. But in all those months, Hoole had told them almost nothing about himself—not even his first name.

During the last few weeks, Hoole had become even more mysterious than usual. He had taken them on several unexplained adventures, often disappearing on long errands without ever telling them where he was going, and leaving them in the hands of their caretaker, the droid DV-9. At first Zak and Tash hadn't thought much about this. After all, Hoole was an anthropologist. It was his job to travel to distant planets and study the species that lived there.

However, Hoole's recent "studies" had taken them to some strange—and very dangerous—places. Tash and Zak soon learned that they had stumbled onto a scheme called Project Starscream, run by someone powerful in the Empire.

But had Uncle Hoole, a simple anthropologist, gotten himself involved in a galaxywide Imperial plot?

That's what Zak and Tash wanted to find out.

They entered the core computer library. It was a large room, lined with video screens and shelves of datadisks. Because it was so early, they had the room to themselves, and Zak quickly dropped into a seat in front of a computer terminal.

"It's easy to access the main computer files," Tash noted. "But the Academy personnel files are under tight security. How do you plan on getting in?"

"With this," Zak said confidently. He held up a small datadisk. "This is a decoder. Deevee had a fancier name for it—"

"A cypher," Tash finished.

"Right, hyperbrain," her brother agreed with a

smirk. "Deevee designed it while trying to break down the computer files we found onboard the *Shroud*."

Tash nodded. On one of their recent journeys, they had acquired a starship called the *Shroud* and discovered that its computers contained coded information about the mysterious Project Starscream.

Zak continued. "This cypher will break through the code and let us look at Uncle Hoole's personnel files. Then we can figure out if he's involved in this Imperial plot."

Punching in a command on the control panel, Zak called up the personnel records. A second later the computer screen flashed the message ACCESS DENIED. SECURITY CLEARANCE REQUIRED.

Zak slid his decoder disk into the computer slot and waited. The computer analyzed the disk and began to process the information. Zak smiled. "Just a few seconds . . ."

The computer screen briefly blinked off, then back on. The words reappeared. ACCESS DENIED. SECURITY CLEARANCE REQUIRED.

"Hey!" Zak exclaimed. "Why didn't it work?"

"Because I disarmed it," said a voice that Zak and Tash knew well.

It was the stern voice of Uncle Hoole.

CHAPTER 2

The two Arrandas turned to face their uncle. Zak looked up into Hoole's dark eyes and his long, grim face. Hoole looked human—only a telltale shade of gray in his skin and his extra-long, delicate hands reminded Zak that his uncle was a member of the Shi'ido species. Of course, Hoole could *look* like anyone or anything he pleased. Zak had seen his uncle transform into creatures as large as a Wookiee and as small as a white rock mouse. Like all members of the Shi'ido species, Hoole was a shape-shifter.

And like other Shi'ido, Hoole usually looked either serious or seriously irritated. Now Zak expected that irritation to explode into anger.

8

To his surprise, Hoole merely removed the datadisk from the computer and said, "I guessed that your curiosity would lead you to the computer files as soon as I had given you some free time. And I have learned over the past month how resourceful you two can be." Zak thought he spotted the hint of a twinkle in Hoole's stern eye. "But my personnel history is not your affair. And I believe that the less you know about recent events, the better off you are."

"But—" Zak began to protest.

"Please do not argue," the Shi'ido stated in a voice that allowed no debate. "There is no time. We will be leaving shortly."

With a swirl of his dark blue robe, Hoole turned and strode from the computer library, with Zak and Tash following. "But we just got here," Zak said. "Where are you taking us now?"

"On vacation," their uncle responded. "Deevee will go with you. I have business where you cannot follow."

Zak and Tash could hardly believe their ears. "A vacation!" Zak exclaimed. "How can we think about relaxing now? We don't even know what Project Starscream is all about—"

"Zak. Tash." Hoole stopped. His Shi'ido features suddenly softened with concern. He looked back and forth between his niece and nephew.

9

"You both must understand that this is not a game. I made a grave mistake when this all began. I should have removed you to safety the moment events turned threatening. My inexperience as a guardian has exposed you to terrible danger, danger that even I do not yet fully understand. The being who created Project Starscream is evil and unpredictable. And I am sure that he and I will meet again."

Tash and Zak looked at one another. On their last adventure, they had come face-to-face with the scientist behind Project Starscream. He was a Shi'ido, just like Hoole. "Uncle Hoole," Tash asked, "who was that scientist?"

Hoole frowned. "His name," the Shi'ido said, "is Borborygmus Gog. He is extremely powerful and *extremely* dangerous. Now let's get going."

"But how do you know him?" Zak asked. "What are you going to do?"

Hoole's face was as still as a durasteel mask. "There are serious questions to be answered. I must continue my research. Now we must hurry." He started down the hall again as he continued to speak. "I am going to bring you somewhere safe, where you will blend in with a crowd of humans and other species your own age. I do not want you to tell anyone where you are going, and once you are there, I do not want you to tell anyone your business."

"Where are we going?" Zak asked as he hurried after his uncle.

Hoole did not bother to turn as he replied, "To Hologram Fun World."

Hours later, on board their ship, the *Shroud,* Zak and the droid DV-9 stood at one of the ship's viewports and watched the transparent dome of Hologram Fun World grow larger as they approached. Fun World was not located on a planet—it had been built inside a transparent dome, suspended in the vacuum of space. Zak estimated that Fun World was about forty kilometers long, the size of a small city. As the *Shroud* drew closer, he made out buildings, mountains—even what looked like an ocean!

"Have you been here before, Deevee?" Zak asked.

Making use of all his humanlike qualities, the silver droid managed to look depressed. "Certainly not," he droned. "As you are well aware, I was a high-level research droid before Master Hoole adopted you and Tash. Visiting an amusement park was not part of my programming." The droid aimed his photoreceptors at the approaching space dome. "Still, Hologram Fun

World is a technological wonder. They say the holographic images look, sound, feel, and even smell like the real objects they imitate."

"Prime," Zak said. "I'll get Tash."

Zak knew just where to find his sister. She could generally be found in her room, reading datastories about the now-extinct Jedi Knights. She believed in the Force and in the powers the Jedi Knights were said to have; she even dreamed of becoming a Jedi herself someday. Until recently Zak had teased Tash about her dream, but during their travels with Hoole, Tash had gotten some strange, unexplainable feelings of dread. She seemed to sense when danger was near, just like (Zak had to admit) the legendary Jedi Knights supposedly could.

But when he reached Tash's cabin, she wasn't reading. She was sitting at her computer terminal.

"We're about to land," Zak said, flopping down on her bed.

The minute he saw the computer screen, Zak knew what Tash had been up to. She had been on the HoloNet, the galaxywide computer network. It was here that Tash had first learned about the Jedi Knights from a mysterious contact, code-named Forceflow. Tash suspected that Forceflow worked for the Rebels, who fought against the Empire. Forceflow had warned her about their last trip, to the planet Gobindi. They should have paid more attention.

"I finally got through to Forceflow," Tash said. "I asked him about Project Starscream and about Hoole."

"Did he know anything?" Zak asked.

Tash pointed to the screen. "Not much. He says that Project Starscream is a top-secret operation run by someone in the Empire. But he says it's not just military. It's scientific."

"We already knew that," Zak replied. "What about Uncle Hoole?"

"Forceflow sent me this." Tash touched a button on her computer and the information on the screen changed. Zak was looking at Hoole's personnel file— the same file they had tried to break into at the Research Academy.

Zak scanned the readout eagerly, but the gleam in his eye faded quickly. According to the files, Hoole had been born on Sh'shuun, the homeworld of the Shi'ido species. He had been an excellent student on Sh'shuun, and eventually he had left his homeworld to study at the Galactic Research Academy, where he became a professor of anthropology. He had dedicated himself to recording the cultural habits of species across the galaxy.

"There's nothing here," he scoffed. "At least nothing we couldn't figure out on our own."

"Look closer," Tash prodded.

Zak scanned the file again and shrugged. He had read everything that appeared on the screen. Then he stopped.

He *hadn't* read what *wasn't* on the screen.

Four years of Hoole's life were missing.

Hoole had left his homeworld. Four years later, he enrolled at the Academy.

"What happened in between?" Zak asked.

Tash shook her head. "Even Forceflow doesn't know. But I'll bet that's why Hoole is so mysterious now."

Zak studied the screen again. "By the way, who *is* this Forceflow?" he wondered out loud. "How does he get so much information?"

"I don't know," his sister replied. "But I'm going to meet him someday. I told Forceflow we were going to Hologram Fun World and that I'd contact him again later."

Zak paused. "Didn't Uncle Hoole warn us not to tell anyone where we were going?"

Tash shrugged. "But this is Forceflow. He's on our side."

———

Tash and Zak reached the cockpit of the *Shroud* just as the ship arrived at Hologram Fun World's docking station. They watched as Hoole guided the ship toward one of the docking latches. There, the *Shroud* would firmly connect to the transparent dome and its airlock, which would allow travelers to enter Fun World without being exposed to the cold, airless void of space.

Hoole deftly touched a thruster control. The *Shroud* nudged forward a few meters and came to rest squarely next to one of the entrance bays. As soon as the ship came to a stop, Hoole turned to his niece and nephew. "This is where we separate. Hologram Fun World is an exciting place—and I know you will be safe here."

"Where are you going?" Zak asked. "When will you be back?"

Hoole paused. "I should be back in a few days. As for where I am going, it is better that you do not know."

The Shi'ido escorted Zak and Tash to the hatchway of the *Shroud*, where Deevee waited, holding two travel cases in his mechanical hands.

Hoole opened the hatchway, which led to a sterile, durasteel airlock. Zak and Tash stepped into the lock and turned to look at their uncle. The stern Shi'ido's face had suddenly softened. He looked almost sad. He raised one hand in a brief goodbye. The outer airlock door closed, and a moment later Zak felt the floor beneath his foot tremble as the *Shroud* launched itself away.

"I hope he knows what he's doing," Zak muttered.

"I think he does," Tash said.

"Master Hoole is quite capable of taking care of himself," Deevee replied. "Now, come. You have an entire holographic world to explore."

Zak, Tash, and Deevee opened the inner door to the transparent space dome and entered Hologram Fun World.

It was like stepping into a dream. Before them, a pathway paved with green gemstones led through a gate shaped like an ancient castle. Beyond the gate, Tash and Zak could see the tops of dozens of buildings gleaming with the polish of modern technology. No two buildings were alike, and thanks to Deevee's many lessons in interplanetary cultures, Zak recognized the architectural styles of at least a hundred different species.

Forest-covered mountains rose up to the very top of the dome, which glimmered fifty kilometers above their heads. Air shuttles full of visitors zoomed this way and that, dodging herds of winged lizards and flocks of blue-winged gibbit birds. Music drifted toward them from different locations within Fun World. Zak heard laughter and shouts of excitement and surprise from the crowds of tourists. He felt as if the entire galaxy had been stuffed inside the transparent walls of the dome.

"Prime," he whispered under his breath.

"No kidding," Tash agreed.

"I suppose," Deevee said, "if one likes this sort of thing."

As they walked toward the old-fashioned stone gate, two young humans on mini-skyhoppers whizzed by overhead. One of them turned a loop in midair, waved at Zak and Tash, then flew away with a laugh.

Maybe this place will be fun after all, Zak thought as he stepped through the gate.

His thoughts were interrupted by a sudden angry roar that shook the entire dome from top to bottom. A blast of stinking breath washed up against Zak like a hot wind. He looked up . . . and up . . . and up.

Into the drooling, fanged mouth of a very hungry rancor.

CHAPTER

Standing on its hind legs, the rancor was ten meters tall. It snorted and its nostrils flared as it let out another blast of fetid breath. The rancor roared, revealing double rows of jagged teeth. Its clawed hands raked the air, and the ground shook as the massive reptilian monster took a single step forward. Its tiny black eyes focused on Zak.

"Get back to the gate!" Tash yelled.

Zak and Tash turned and ran. The rancor charged after them, its footsteps thundering down the path. With each step, the giant predator cut the distance to his fleeing prey in half.

Zak looked over his shoulder and noticed that

Deevee had not moved. He stood directly in the rancor's path, totally motionless. Tash and Zak stopped in midstride.

"Deevee!" Tash yelled.

"He may have short-circuited," Zak guessed. "We've got to go back and get him."

"It's too late!"

Tash was right. The rancor reached the droid, reared back its head, and lunged. Deevee did not even flinch as two thousand kilograms of flesh-eating monster fell on him.

And passed right through him.

Zak and Tash gasped in surprise. The rancor swept right through Deevee as though it were made of smoke. It stopped a few steps beyond the droid, then, with an ear-shattering roar, the rancor vanished like an illusion or . . ."

"A hologram!" Zak guessed. "That rancor wasn't real at all."

"Correct," said Deevee, coming back down the path for his two charges.

"It was real enough to fool me," Tash said with a nervous laugh. "I thought that thing was going to crush you, Deevee."

The droid simulated a bored sigh. "That's because you lack my delicate instrumentation. I knew instantly that the rancor was not real because it did not register on my sensors. There were no life-readings emanating from the hologram, so my program ignored it. It wasn't real." The droid waved one mechanical hand across the scene before them. "Hologram Fun World might be exciting for humans and other species that rely on their biological senses, but for a droid, well, it's rather boring."

"Boring!" Zak exclaimed. He watched a Star Dragon pass overhead, curling its way gently through the air. "This place is anything but boring. Let's check out some of the rides."

"Not yet," Deevee insisted. "We should find lodging first and then—"

But Zak had already started toward the nearest attraction.

He hurried up the steps to a building that resembled a small temple, with white columns around the outside. An electronic sign at the top of the steps announced the attraction in a dozen of the galaxy's most common languages. "Hall of Reflection," Zak read. *Hall of Reflection?* Zak wondered. *Is this some sort of meditation chamber?*

He peeked inside, but the entranceway was dark. Using his hands, Zak felt his way down a narrow hall that opened up into empty space. Zak took a few more steps before he heard a click as automatic glow rods activated, flooding the room with light.

He was surrounded by a dozen gruesome trolls with hunched backs, hair that seemed to explode out of their heads in spikes, and twisted faces.

"Agh!" he shouted in surprise.

"Agh!" a dozen hunchbacks shouted at the same time.

Zak turned to run, and the hunchbacks turned with him. As he lunged back into the safety of the hallway, the hunchbacks vanished without a sound.

Zak stopped running. This place was becoming stranger by the minute. Curious, he turned and stuck his head back into the lighted room.

A dozen gruesome trolls also poked their heads out through a dozen doors. When Zak raised an eyebrow, so did they. When he scratched his head in confusion, they did, too.

"Hall of Reflection," he said. "I get it."

Zak stepped boldly into the room and stared at the trolls—which were actually twelve images of him. He was surrounded by twelve mirrors that took his reflection and warped it into something almost unrecognizable. He laughed out loud, and his reflected image suddenly became even more ridiculous. One of its eyes bulged as large as a port hole, while the other shrank to a tiny, wrinkled pit in his face.

"It's an improvement," Tash said wryly. She and Deevee had followed him into the Hall of Reflection and were standing at the edge of the hallway. "I especially like your hair."

"Very funny," Zak replied. "Let's see what it does to you."

Tash stepped into the room, and the gruesome trolls were instantly joined by twelve gnarled crones. Tash's long, braided blond hair looked like a tentacle writhing out of the back of her head, and her eyes shrank back into her brow as her chin swelled up and out.

"This is the most amazing funhouse mirror I've ever seen," she said. When she spoke, her reflections' enormous jaws flapped wildly.

"I'm programmed to imitate human functions, but I'm not sure I comprehend this sort of humor," Deevee confessed. "These trick mirrors intentionally distort one's image. And that is funny?"

Zak rolled his eyes. "Let's see if there's more."

They searched the mirrored room until they found a door—hidden behind one of the twelve reflections. Stepping through it, Tash and Zak entered a mirror maze. Pieces of their reflections were everywhere—

sometimes only their feet were visible, and sometimes only their heads. Sometimes the reflections were true, and sometimes the Fun World mirrors twisted their images into shapes that were stretched, squeezed, crushed, or swollen to galactic proportions. Zak even found a set of mirrors that transformed him into an alien. In one mirror, his face stretched out into a snout and his ears drooped down. Even his skin changed color, until he looked like a pudgy Ortolan.

"This is excellent!" he called out to Tash, who was walking in the other direction.

In the next mirror, his entire face folded in on itself and his skin swelled into the tough, leathery hide of a somewhat Zaklike Kitonak.

Zak stepped up to the next mirror in the hallway. This image was human and very handsome—but taller than he was, with smooth dark skin, a carefully trimmed mustache, and a dashing smile.

Now this is more like it, Zak thought. He struck a swashbuckler's pose.

But instead of imitating the pose, the reflection reached out and grabbed him by the shoulder.

CHAPTER

"Help!" Zak cried as the hand clutched at his shirt.

"Relax," said a smooth, confident voice. "I didn't mean to startle you."

The image stepped forward, and Zak realized with relief that he *hadn't* been looking at another reflection. He'd been looking at a living, breathing human being.

"You nearly made me jump into hyperspace," he said, trying to calm his pounding heart.

The man flashed a roguish smile. His age was hard to guess. He might have been twenty or forty. He had the casual confidence of a traveler who'd been everywhere and done everything, but also the sly look of a young scoundrel with his sharp eyes on a new opportunity for riches.

"Sorry about that," the man said in a slow drawl. "You almost ran into me."

"Zak! Are you all right?" Tash yelled. A dozen reflections of his sister appeared before the real Tash finally turned the corner, with Deevee close behind her. Tash stopped when she saw her brother talking to a stranger. "Oh. Hello."

"And hello to you," the man said. He took Tash's hand gently in his. "I was just about to introduce myself to your friend . . . Zak, is it? My name is Lando Calrissian. A pleasure."

"That's my sister, Tash," Zak said.

"And I am DV-9, the caretaker for these young humans," said Deevee, inserting himself into the conversation. His program bristled at the intrusion of a stranger.

"I thought he was another reflection until he grabbed me," Zak explained.

Tash nodded. "This place is pretty confusing. I was just around the corner when you yelled, but it took me all this time to find the path."

"Yeah, it's prime here," Zak said. "No wonder Hologram Fun World is so popular."

Lando's ears perked up. "You really like it here?"

Zak laughed. "We've only just arrived, but so far, so good."

"Listen," Lando said, "I'm a businessman. I'm looking for, well, investments, and I'm considering buying part ownership in Fun World. But before I do, I want to get the opinions of some Fun World visitors—especially kids your age."

"And?" Deevee asked. His analytical computer brain told him this was leading somewhere.

Lando turned his charm on Deevee. "And I was hoping Zak and Tash would let me tour the park with them. That way I can get an honest feel for their reactions. Which parts of the Fun World are actually fun, and which ones aren't. Things like that."

"I'm afraid I can't allow that," Deevee replied. "I have been charged with the care of these humans, and my master would not appreciate their taking up with a complete stranger."

Lando spread his hands out innocently and smiled again. "You do me an injustice. I haven't been doubted like this since the Battle of Tanaab."

"You were at the Battle of Tanaab?" Zak asked. He had a passion for starships, and loved to read about famous starship battles.

Lando shrugged with an air of false humility. "I played a small part in that skirmish."

"I hear those Norulackian pirates were using supercharged Incom BG2300 engines," Zak said. "Were they really as fast as—"

"Excuse me," Deevee interrupted. "But as I said, I am responsible for these children, and I am programmed to be wary of strangers."

Lando frowned. "I see. Well, if you change your mind, I'll be in the park for a few days. I'm staying at a visitor's lodge called the Gravity Well. It's near the center of Fun World."

Lando flashed a dashing smile and turned away.

"Deevee, that was rude," Tash scolded.

Deevee stiffened. "Tash, after the number of unsettling events that have befallen us recently, I suggest we remain cautious of strangers."

"Actually," Zak said thoughtfully, "seeing Fun World with Lando might not be such a bad idea. If Uncle Hoole's worried that someone might be looking for two humans and a droid, then maybe they're not looking for *three* humans and a droid. Seeing the park with Lando might throw anyone trying to track us down off the trail."

Deevee considered. "I'm not sure I agree, Zak. Still, your logic is sound—"

"Great!" Zak said without letting the droid finish. "Hey, Lando!" he called, chasing after the dashing entrepreneur.

Zak, Tash, and Deevee caught up with their new companion, who led them through a dizzying maze of rides, attractions, and crowds until they reached the visitor's lodge called the Gravity Well. Groups of tourists poured in and out of its doors, and the four newcomers easily blended in with the mob.

"What's that?" Zak asked, pointing to a large structure across the courtyard from the Gravity Well. The building's durasteel walls were so well-polished that they acted like mirrors, reflecting the amazing sights and activities of the park.

"That's the administration building," Lando replied. "I have some meetings there with the park owner tomorrow."

The Twi'lek clerk at the check-in counter knew Calrissian by name, and the attendant droid fawned over Lando as it showed them to their rooms.

Since it was getting late in the day, Deevee suggested that they get some rest before heading into Fun World tomorrow. Tash immediately settled herself in to read a datadisk on her datapad. Zak, however, was restless. An entire holographic galaxy lay just outside his room, but he could not get to it until morning. After several hours of watching boring holoprograms, he wandered into the hallway, down to Lando's room, and buzzed for entry.

"Come!" said a smooth voice, and the automatic door slid open.

Zak saw Lando sitting at a table across from three people. He recognized the Twi'lek from the reception desk, who sat next to a very large humanoid. If he was human, he was the ugliest human Zak had ever seen. Part of his face was hidden by a ragged scarf. Beside him sat a two-mouthed Ithorian, also known as a Hammerhead.

"Zak!" Lando said with a friendly grin. "Nice to see you. Come on in. We'll be done here in a minute."

The humanoid growled, "Just play your cards, Calrissian."

"Patience, Dengar," Lando said happily. "I'm just being sociable to my young friend here." Lando turned his brilliant smile on Zak. "Have a seat. Ever watched a game of sabacc?"

Zak shook his head and sat down.

He had heard of sabacc, of course. It was the most popular gambling game in the galaxy. High-stakes sabacc games were played for thousands of credits, or the ownership of star cruisers and even whole planets.

The center of the table was covered in piles of multi-colored chips, and all the players looked anxious—except Lando. The Twi'lek nervously rubbed one of the two thick tentacles that grew out of the back of his head. The human, Dengar, scowled down at his cards. The Ithorian hummed anxiously in stereo out of his two mouths. Lando Calrissian yawned.

"Bet's to you, Calrissian," Dengar growled.

"Ah, yes," Lando replied with an air of boredom. "Let's make it interesting, shall we? I bet a thousand credits." Lando took a stack of sabacc chips from his personal collection and dumped them into the central pile.

"A thousand credits!" the Twi'lek moaned. "You've already taken everything I had. I can't bet that."

Lando smiled. "Then I guess you're out."

The Twi'lek slapped his cards down on the table and stroked his tentacled head furiously.

The Ithorian piped a grating, worried note out of its two mouths and laid its cards down on the table, dropping out of the game.

"I'm in," Dengar growled. He tossed more chips into the pile. He had only a few left. "Time to deal the last card."

Lando reached over to a small box—an electronic shuffler that randomly mixed the cards—and pulled out two. The first one he gave to Dengar. The second he kept for himself. As he added the card to his collection, Lando's grin widened. "Ah, sweet starlight," he crooned. He picked up another pile of chips. "I bet another thousand."

"Stang!" Dengar swore. "That bet'll wipe me out. But I gotta see your cards."

Lando looked Dengar right in the eye. "Then you better toss your credits in the pot."

Zak watched Dengar and Lando. Dengar fingered his last few chips and glared at his opponent, while Lando merely smiled and waited calmly. His hands were poised over his cards, ready to reveal his hand. Everything about him promised victory.

Finally Dengar made his decision. "I'm out!" he roared, throwing his cards onto the table.

Lando sighed. "All right." With a grand flourish, he swept all the chips into his pile.

"Wait a minute," Dengar growled. "Show me your cards."

"I don't have to show you anything," the gambler replied. "You went out. That means I don't have to reveal my hand."

"Show me your cards!" Dengar roared. He reached for the blaster on his hip.

Quicker than lightspeed, Lando pulled a small black

object from his sleeve. It was pointed at Dengar's heart before the angry man could draw his own weapon. "Get out of here, Dengar," he said softly. "Before my little hold-out blaster puts a hole in you big enough to fly a star freighter through."

Dengar continued to scowl, but he carefully moved his hand away from his gun. "You ain't heard the last of me, Calrissian," he promised as he backed out of the room. He was followed by the Twi'lek and the Ithorian. Only when they were gone did Lando show any sign of nervousness, releasing a huge sigh of relief as he put his hold-out blaster on the table.

"Sorry you had to see that, Zak," the gambler said as his smile returned. "Sometimes these games get out of hand if all the players aren't gentles like myself."

"Why didn't you want to show him your cards?" Zak asked. "I mean, if you had such a winning hand . . ."

He turned over Lando's cards and gasped. He was no expert card player, but he knew enough to see that Lando had the worst hand possible!

"Y-You would have lost!" Zak stammered. "You were bluffing the whole time! It's lucky he didn't stay in the game."

"Kid, luck's got nothing to do with it," Lando boasted. "Here's your first lesson in sabacc and in life, my young friend. Nothing is what it seems." He picked up his small hold-out blaster—and Zak gasped again. The "blaster" was actually a small, harmless remote-control device.

"This is the homing beacon to my ship," the roguish gambler said with a laugh. "As I said, nothing is what it seems. Want to learn how to play?"

Before he knew it, Zak was deep into a lesson in sabacc gambling. He learned how to bluff an opponent into thinking he had a good hand, and to guess when his opponent was bluffing, too.

"A good rule to follow," Lando explained, "is that if the other guy is acting normal under unusual circumstances, you can bet he's bluffing."

Lando showed Zak how to operate the small electronic shuffler by inserting the seventy-two cards and squeezing the grip. Lando made it look easy, but when Zak tried it, he found out that the electronic shuffler was more complicated than it seemed.

"Watch out!" Lando yelled. He ducked just in time as all seventy-two cards came flying out of the shuffler's chute in a rain of plastic.

"Sorry," Zak said.

"The shuffler is touch-sensitive," Lando explained. "It takes practice. Keep that one until you get it down."

"Thanks!" Zak replied. "And thanks for showing me how to play sabacc."

"My pleasure," the gambler replied. "Just remember that tomorrow you'll return the favor when we tour Hologram Fun World together."

The next day, Tash, Zak, and Deevee met Lando in front of the Gravity Well, and together they plunged into the holographic craziness of Fun World.

There were crowds of people everywhere. Zak spotted members of a hundred familiar species in the first hour, and a hundred other species he'd never seen before. They strolled past magic shows that made entire audiences vanish for a full minute, and holodrama theaters where the characters in the stories were projected ten meters high.

But the greatest attractions were the rides. Zak and Tash hoverskied down the side of an exploding volcano. They entered the Star Chamber, an enormous room that contained a hologram of the entire galaxy. In the chamber, the two Arrandas walked across the cosmos, striding past planets shrunk to the size of blumfruit and stars no larger than melons. Outside, they hopped onto the back of a passing Star Dragon and rode it around the top of Fun World's giant protective dome. The Star Dragon dropped them off at the shores of an inlet that led out to an impossibly large ocean. The digital sign at the entrance to the beach read: WELCOME TO SWEETSAND LAGOON.

"Isn't this amazing?" Tash yelled.

"I could stay here forever!" her brother replied.

"I'm beginning to think this might be a good investment," Lando murmured.

"It's really all an illusion," Deevee hastened to point out. "In reality, most of what you are seeing is not actually there."

"Don't ruin it," Zak interrupted. "We know they're holograms, too, but it's still fun. Can't you just pretend?"

"I am a scientific research droid," Deevee sniffed. "Once I acquire information, I cannot simply *forget* it."

"Your loss." Zak shrugged and turned to his sister. "Let's go for a swim."

Jumping off the dragon's back, they swam out to a waiting Whaladon—an enormous fish the size of a starship. As the Whaladon floated patiently on the water's surface, Zak and Tash crawled up along its scaly, barnacle-covered side to its back, then hung on for dear life. With a swipe of its ten-meter tail, the Whaladon sped off on a cruise along the holographic shore.

Finally the Whaladon deposited them back at the

Sweetsand Lagoon. Lando was just asking them which rides they liked best when he was interrupted by an ear-shattering roar.

The rancor had returned.

Instinctively they all turned as the carnivore charged at them. But no one ran. They watched calmly as the rancor pounced on them, raking its huge claws toward their bodies.

The claws passed through them as harmlessly as a breeze.

"It must roam around the park, scaring the heck out of the new visitors," Zak guessed.

Together they left the lagoon and wandered back in among the attractions. Down one of Fun World's side streets, they saw a small building with a sign, THE ANYWHERE ROOM.

"What's this?" Zak asked the attendant droid who stood at the door.

"The Anywhere Room," replied the droid in a pleasant voice. "This room will take you to your heart's desire. See the flaming falls on the fire rivers of Sittana. Sit on the Emperor's throne. Visit your homeworld. Whatever you desire, The Anywhere Room will take you there."

"Even—" Tash said hesitantly, "even if your homeworld was destroyed?"

"If it ever existed, it's stored in here," the droid said with a mechanical jerk toward the door. "We have holograms of every known planet in the galaxy."

"Tash," Zak said, guessing his sister's thoughts. "We could go back to Alderaan. We could see our house again!"

Brother and sister came forward, just to the doorway. With just one step, they could enter the room. They could revisit the planet that the Empire had destroyed. They could actually go home.

Neither took another step.

"We could go home," Tash said. "But it wouldn't be real. It would just be a hologram."

Zak nodded. "I don't want to."

They turned away.

"You're from Alderaan?" Lando asked. Like many people in the galaxy, he had heard that the Empire's doomsday weapon, the Death Star, had blasted Alderaan to rubble. "I'm sorry."

"Thanks," Tash managed to say.

Zak said nothing. He'd been happy a few minutes before. For a brief moment, he'd forgotten about his parents and his homeworld. He'd even forgotten about Project Starscream. Now it all came back, and he needed to take his mind off it.

Farther down the lane, Zak saw a small-domed

building with a sign outside that announced: HOLOGRAM FUN WORLD'S LATEST ATTRACTION: THE NIGHTMARE MACHINE! He went to investigate.

The only entrance to the building was a tall archway, which was being polished by a maintenance droid. Zak read another sign. This one was placed over the archway: FACE THE ULTIMATE FEAR . . . IF YOU DARE. Zak could not resist a challenge. He started to enter the dome.

"Pardon me, young gentle," said the boxy maintenance droid. "This attraction is still under construction. It is not ready for visitors."

"Okay," Zak said, still curious. He wanted to see just what The Nightmare Machine could possibly be. "You missed a spot right over there." He pointed to a portion of the wall five meters distant.

"Thank you," replied the droid, turning to investigate.

While its back was turned, Zak entered The Nightmare Machine.

He stepped into a small hallway lit only by dim maintenance glowpanels. They were just bright enough for Zak to see a few tools, such as hydrospanners and sonic hammers, strewn on the ground among extra pieces of durasteel and wiring.

Zak was about to leave when he heard a noise at the

far end of the hallway. Consumed with curiosity, Zak walked quietly toward the noise. Light came from a room at the end of the hall.

A voice spoke, cold and sharp as a vibroblade. "Get them on the tables. Hurry!"

Carefully keeping himself in the shadows of the hallway, Zak peered into the room.

And found himself looking into the evil, gray face of the scientist who ran Project Starscream.

Zak was looking into the eyes of Borborygmus Gog himself.

CHAPTER 5

It took Zak one terrifying moment to realize that Gog could not see him in the shadows. The Shi'ido scientist was standing next to a large black transport cube. Before him were two medical tables. Gog was looking to the left of the door, where four men in black uniforms dragged two young humans toward the tables.

Zak recognized the two human kids he had seen flying the hoverskis yesterday. They struggled to break free, but they were gagged and their arms were bound; they were no match for the four men who lifted them onto the tables.

Zak felt fear trickle down his spine like icy-cold water. How could Gog possibly be at Hologram Fun

World? Had he followed them? If so, why hadn't he captured them already?

Zak's heart pounded. He couldn't just watch as Gog tormented two helpless kids. He had to do something.

Before he could move, Gog spoke. "Now," said the Shi'ido. "Let us see if our little experiment works."

He pressed a button on the side of the large black cube and a panel slid open with a hiss.

No, the panel hadn't hissed. Something *inside* the transport cube had hissed. From the shadows of the container, something shuffled forward.

First, two arms appeared. The hands were long, with thin, splayed fingers. The arms themselves were terribly thin, like skin stretched tightly over dried bones. And each arm had two sets of elbows, which made them quiver and swerve in weird directions.

Next came the creature's head. Its face was vaguely human, but the head was enormous and round. Above two red eyes, the skull was crisscrossed with hundreds of wormlike veins, as though the creature's brain were about to push up through the skull. Its lips were thin and tightly shut, and the corners of its mouth stretched back almost to its tiny ears.

Zak was grossed out. He stifled a cry of fear as the creature crawled spiderlike out of its box and loomed over the two victims. It looked at Gog, who nodded at it. Then the creature opened its mouth. Instead of a tongue, two tentacles leaped out, wriggling in the air. One tentacle struck the top of each captive's head and attached itself. The two teens stiffened in shock, then fainted.

Zak gasped. It was a tiny sound, but it was enough to turn the heads of Gog and his henchmen. The Shi'ido's dark eyes stared directly at Zak, and the scientist smiled cruelly.

Zak didn't hesitate. He turned and ran as fast as his feet would carry him. He burst out of The Nightmare Machine, past the bustling maintenance droid, and into the brightly lit air of Fun World, where Tash, Deevee, and Lando were waiting.

"Zak, we were just looking for you—" Tash said.

"We've got to get out of here!" Zak interrupted. "He's here! He's here!"

"Who's here?" Deevee asked.

Zak pulled on Tash's arm. "The scientist! Gog! The one behind Project Starscream!"

"That's impossible!" Tash said. "Why would he be here?"

Zak looked back toward The Nightmare Machine. He was surprised to see that no one had followed him, but that didn't ease his fears. "I don't know. Maybe he followed us. But he's here. And he's got some kind of . . . of creature with him!"

Lando was confused. "Project Starscream? Gog? What's going on?"

"We've got to get out of here!" Zak insisted.

"How?" Deevee asked calmly. "We have no starship. Master Hoole will not return for several days."

"Will someone please tell me what's going on?" Lando insisted.

Tash, remembering her uncle's warning to tell no one, said carefully, "It looks like Zak saw someone in The Nightmare Machine that we think may be a—a criminal."

Lando considered. "Maybe I can help. I know the baron administrator of Hologram Fun World. He can help you with this criminal, and I know he'll ensure your safety."

A few minutes later, Lando brought Zak, Tash, and Deevee to the doors of the administrative building at the center of Fun World. Zak could see his own reflection in the gleaming durasteel walls as they entered the automatic doors.

Lando took them to the top floor, ten levels above ground. The entire top floor of the administrative building was taken up by a single circular office, with windows facing in all directions. Star Dragons swooped around the top of the building, and hoverjet racers hurtled passed the windows of the baron administrator's office. From that office, they could look out over the entire Fun World.

"Not bad," Lando whistled appreciatively. "I could get used to this."

The baron administrator was a man named Danna Fajji. He was short and chubby, with jovial red cheeks and a scruffy red beard at the end of his chin.

Leaving out all references to Project Starscream, Zak told Fajji of the horror he'd seen in The Nightmare Machine—of the Shi'ido scientist and the kidnapped teens. Even Lando shuddered as Zak described the horrible, double-jointed brain creature, its tentacled mouth, and its enormous head. "It was huge, and covered in wriggling veins!"

Danna Fajji only chuckled. "I assure you that everything is under control," he replied.

"But there are two kids being tortured back there!" Zak insisted. "And there's a monster!"

Again Fajji smiled. "Please, believe me. I'll even take you back there myself."

"Come on. We might as well check it out," Lando told Zak.

"Well . . . okay," Zak agreed, deciding that not much could happen with Lando there. The chubby red-haired man led them all back through the eye-dazzling attractions of Fun World until they reached The Nightmare Machine.

"We shouldn't go in," Zak warned. "We should have security people here, or something."

Fajji shook his head. "It's unnecessary. Watch."

Fajji stepped boldly into the domed building. Tash followed him, with Deevee and Lando bringing up the rear.

Zak hesitated. Maybe he had been fooled by a hologram. That's what this place was all about, after all. He looked around Fun World. Sounds of laughter and chords of happy music floated toward him from all directions. He looked to his left, toward the sunny lagoon with its sparkling water. This was definitely not a place to be afraid of. Shaking his head at his own silliness, he hurried after the others.

The minute he stepped inside, Zak could tell that something was different. The door at the end of the hall was wide open now, and he could see into the room beyond. There were no examination tables, no henchmen, no black transport cube, and certainly no mad Shi'ido scientist.

The room was empty.

"You see," Danna Fajji said. "I told you everything was under control."

"I . . . I don't get it," Zak said. "I saw him. I saw that . . . that creature as clearly as I see you standing there."

"Zak, are you sure?" Tash asked.

"I thought I was sure," Zak said, stepping into the room to look around. "But how could they have packed everything up so quickly? I don't get it." He looked at Danna Fajji. "I guess you're right. There's nothing to be afraid of."

Danna Fajji grinned. "Oh. I wouldn't say *that*."

As he spoke, the lights went out and Zak was plunged into complete darkness.

"Tash! Deevee!" he called out in fear. "Lando!"

There was no answer but a sudden soft sound coming from the floor around him.

Scratch, scratch. Scratch, scratch.

"Tash?" he said faintly.

Scratch, scratch.

Zak heard the skitter of tiny feet. *Thousands* of tiny feet. They scraped along the ground all around him. Something brushed across his foot. Then again, and again.

Scratch, scratch, scratch!

Something crawled up his pant leg. Panicked, Zak

46

tried to brush it away, and felt something soft and hairy and many-legged cling to the back of his hand. Then it started to crawl up his arm.

More of the skittering creatures were crawling up his pant legs. He felt them crawling inside his pant legs and inside his shirtsleeves, pushing their way up his shirt, crawling out from under his collar and scrambling around the back of his neck. Zak wildly thrashed his arms and legs about, trying to get the horrible creatures off him.

He felt something tugging and biting at his hair. Zak opened his mouth to scream, and a dozen hairy legs scrambled past his lips.

CHAPTER

Zak stumbled around the pitch-black room, crushing little insect bodies beneath his feet, scratching and pulling at the creatures that covered his body.

"Get off! Get off me!" he cried, spitting the creatures out of his mouth. Using his hands, Zak blindly groped around until he found the wall, then began searching for the door. But it was impossible to concentrate—small, hairy insects were crawling through his hair and across his eyes.

Just when Zak thought he couldn't stand it anymore, a door opened in the darkness. A wide beam of light poured into the room, and through it stepped Danna Fajji, Baron Administrator of Hologram Fun World.

"End simulation," Fajji said calmly.

Quicker than lightspeed, the feeling of creepy-crawly legs vanished and the lights went on. Zak looked at the floor, expecting to see bloodstains and the squashed bodies of the creatures he had stepped on, but the floor looked like it had just been polished.

"What—what *was* that?" Zak gasped.

"That," Danna Fajji explained, "was a hologram of one of your fears."

Zak shuddered. "Tash, Lando, did you feel them, too? Little crawling things. They were everywhere."

Tash shook her head. She looked a little pale. "No—no crawling things. Heights. I was on this tiny ledge, hanging over a bottomless pit. I was just about to fall when the lights came on!"

Lando stroked his mustache thoughtfully. Whatever he had seen, he kept it to himself.

"What is this place?" Zak asked.

"Let us step outside and I'll tell you," Danna Fajji replied. As soon as all five of them were outside the building, Fajji proudly announced, "This is The Nightmare Machine. It's the latest addition to Hologram Fun World."

"What does it do?" Tash asked. "I mean, besides scare people."

Fajji laughed. "Nothing! That's what it does. It's The

Nightmare Machine. Once you enter this room, The Nightmare Machine scans your mind for your greatest fears. Then it shows them to you."

"That doesn't sound like fun to me," Lando said. "Who would pay to be scared?"

"Actually, Master Calrissian," Deevee answered, "being scared is a popular form of entertainment in many cultures. Humans actually pay to take heart-stopping roller-coaster rides, watch frightening holoprograms, and even read horror stories. It's quite beyond my capacity."

"Exactly," Danna Fajji agreed. "People like to be scared. And this machine takes fright to new heights. It reaches into your brain, pulls out your worst fears, and re-creates them in a hologram."

"Then . . . what I saw earlier . . . with the scientist and The Nightmare Machine creature . . ." Zak began.

". . . was just The Nightmare Machine doing its job," Danna Fajji said. "Obviously the image of this scientist represents something scary in your mind, and The Nightmare Machine just made it real."

"It makes sense," Tash whispered to her brother. "That *is* what was on our minds."

Zak shook his head. "But what I saw earlier was so real. I mean, these little hairy legs in the dark were bad"—he shivered, remembering—"but it wasn't as realistic as the scientist and the monster and those two kids."

The baron administrator nodded. "Unfortunately you're right. The program isn't always consistent. The Nightmare Machine still has a few bugs to be worked out. That's why it's not open to the public yet."

"Excuse me, sir," Deevee said. "But did you say the program scans the brains of beings and records their worst fears? As far as I know, no one has the technology to read minds. Only certain telepathic beings can do that."

Fajji puffed up proudly. "We've broken that technology barrier."

"Really?" Lando said, intrigued.

"How does it work?" asked Zak. "Can we see the machinery?"

"No," Fajji replied quickly. "That's classified information. We don't want anyone copying our inventions, you know."

"So once you're inside, how does the ride end?" Lando asked.

"There are only two ways," the baron administrator said. "The first is, you stay through to the end of the holograms. The Nightmare Machine will scan your brain and put you through a series of increasingly

51

frightening scenes. If you can get to the last one—your own ultimate fear—then you win the game and it ends. If you can't take it, then all you have to do is say 'End simulation!' and the program will end." He paused. "So, now that you know what you're getting into, do you want to go for another ride?"

Zak and Tash looked at each other. "Let's do it," Tash said.

"Sure," Zak replied reluctantly.

Danna Fajji escorted Zak and Tash into the building, with Lando and Deevee following behind them. "Enjoy yourselves," Fajji said with a smile, and guided the two Arrandas into the fearful room.

Zak had hardly taken his first step before the scene around him changed. The room vanished, and Zak found himself in the middle of a wide field, standing on his hovering skimboard. Tash was standing behind him, clinging to him to keep her balance on the narrow antigravity board. Before Zak could speak, Lando and Deevee jumped onto the board as well.

"It's too heavy!" Zak said as the skimboard wobbled. "It's going to sink."

"It better not!" Lando shouted. "Because we're being chased by Cyborrean battle dogs!'

Zak turned and saw a pack of massive, thick-bodied

dogs with wide jaws and short blood-red hair charging toward them. They howled viciously.

Instinctively Zak hit the skimboard's accelerator. But the hoverboard was slowed down by too much weight, and it lurched forward sluggishly.

"C'mon, Zak!" Tash yelled, "get this thing going before it—*agh*!"

Before Tash could finish her sentence, the first dog reached the skimboard. Its powerful jaws clamped down on the back of Tash's tunic, and one twist of its thick neck pulled her from the safety of the board.

"Tash!" Zak yelled.

His sister hit the ground hard. She rolled to one side and tried to scramble to her feet. But it was too late. The battle dogs attacked, and Tash fell under a pile of bristling fur and sharp fangs.

"They're killing her!" Deevee wailed.

"Tash!" Lando called out.

Zak knew he had to stop the battle dogs before they tore Tash apart. "End simulation!" he ordered.

But the simulation did not end.

CHAPTER

Tash could hardly be seen beneath the swarm of savage dogs.

"End simulation!" Zak cried out. Tears of fear and frustration burned in his eyes. "End simulation!"

It was no use. The program would not stop.

Without thinking, Zak leaped from the skimboard. He had been afraid of the invisible insects earlier, and he was afraid of the battle dogs now. But none of that compared to his fear of losing his sister. He charged into the dog pack, trying to pull them off Tash.

One of the dogs turned and growled, baring a mouth full of sharp fangs. It crouched down, ready to spring at Zak's throat.

"End simulation," Tash's calm voice stated.

The entire pack of battle dogs melted away. So did the field in which Zak stood. He was back inside The Nightmare Machine again. Tash was standing across the room from him.

"T-Tash!" Zak sputtered, caught between fear and confusion. "You're okay! But . . . but I thought we were in the hologram together. You were being mauled by Cyborrean battle dogs."

"It wasn't me," his sister replied. "It must have been a hologram of me. There weren't any battle dogs in my hologram."

"Mine was terrible," Zak muttered. "I tried to end the simulation, but it wouldn't respond. I wonder if that's another bug that needs to be worked out."

"Well, we've spent enough time here, in any event," Lando concluded. "Let's tour the rest of the park, shall we?"

They left The Nightmare Machine and walked out into the artificial light of Fun World.

"I'd like to visit the lagoon again," Tash suggested.

"All right," Zak agreed. "It's over here." He turned to his left.

"No it's not," Tash laughed. "It's over here." She pointed to the right. Between two buildings, they could just see a thin blue strip of water.

Zak shook his head. "That's funny, I could have sworn I saw it over on this side."

Deevee tilted his head understandingly. "The large number of holographic projections in this space could confuse a species. Unless, of course, one happens to be a droid of superior quality."

"Right, Deevee," Tash groaned. "Let's go."

But Zak wasn't listening. As he looked around to get his bearings, he caught a glimpse of something disturbingly familiar. A large, pale creature clung to the side of a wall, its double-jointed arms and legs twisted at bizarre angles. Zak saw the flashing blood-red eyes and an enormous head. But by the time he'd turned to look directly at the thing, it was gone.

"What's wrong?" Tash asked.

"Did you see that?"

She looked around. "See what?"

Zak didn't respond. The creature had been clinging to the outside wall of the Hall of Reflection. Zak thought he'd seen it slip inside.

"Zak?" Tash prompted him.

"I think I saw it," he replied. "The creature I saw in The Nightmare Machine."

Deevee heaved an electronic sigh. "Zak, we've been through this already. That was merely a hologram."

"Maybe. Maybe not," Zak said. He started toward the building.

He didn't have time to argue. By the time he convinced them to follow, the creature would be long gone.

Zak reached the steps of the Hall of Reflection. The building looked basically the same as it did yesterday, yet somehow different. It was darker and more shadowy. Zak did not pause to dwell on the change. He plunged into the mirror maze.

Inside, there was no sign of the brain creature. But Zak decided to keep looking.

He saw his own image reflected dozens of times. Just as before, the reflections were distorted, but now they were even more hideous. Zak wasn't just reflected as a silly-looking troll. Now he looked like a monster. With each twist and turn that took him deeper into the hall of mirrors, Zak's reflection became more hideous.

Finally, as he reached what he guessed was the center of the maze, Zak saw an image that made him gag. He was looking at his own face, but his skin had melted and hung from his cheeks in sagging clumps. His eyes had sunk back into their sockets so that they looked like holes in his skull. His arms had grown twice as long. His knuckles dragged on the floor. His elbows reached down to his knees, which were now jointed in the opposite direction so that they pointed backward instead of forward.

"Agh!" he cried. He reached out to touch the glass that held his distorted image. His reflection jiggled as it moved and reached forward in the same motion. As Zak touched the glass, his reflection touched the glass at exactly the same point, and the whole image shimmered into a blur.

When the mirror cleared again, Zak was looking at a perfect image of his true self. He saw his own messy brown hair and his own face. His reflection was grinning wickedly. That was odd, because Zak didn't think he was smiling.

He tried to raise one hand to touch his face, but his arm felt heavy and awkward. With some effort he managed to lift his hand . . . only to find that it was as long and deformed as the horrible image he'd seen before.

He tried to step back from the mirror but stumbled.

His own knees bent backward. Zak dragged his two clumsy hands up to his face, and felt the skin hanging limp and soft from his cheeks. He let out a wail.

Zak had turned into a monster.

CHAPTER

8

Zak tried to speak, but his words were garbled and lost in the folds of melted flesh around his lips.

"Zak?" Tash's voice drifted in from outside the Hall of Reflection. "Zak, are you in here?"

Trying to balance on his backward legs, Zak staggered through the maze. The mirrors reflected his own hideous form back at him.

"Zak!" Tash called again. "I'm coming in to look for you!"

No! Zak thought. *If Tash comes in here she'll be changed, too.* Zak struggled to make his mouth work properly.

"Nnnaaa!" he bellowed. "Shtay bach!"

"Zak?" Tash's voice deepened with concern. "Is that you? You're scaring me!"

Zak could not stop slurring his words. "Don commm ind!"

He had to do something! Turning his head, Zak caught a glimpse of himself—his *real* self—in one of the mirrors.

"Gotja!" he mumbled. He reached out and touched the mirror. Just as before, the reflection shimmered. When it stopped, Zak looked down at his own hand. It looked normal.

"Zak!" Lando called out.

"I'm coming!" he replied in his own clear voice. "Don't touch the mirrors!"

Zak carefully wound his way back through the maze until he reached the exit where the others had stopped.

"We're over here!" Tash called out. "What's going on?"

"M-My reflection!" he explained breathlessly. "The mirrors stole it. They changed me into a—a monster."

Lando raised an eyebrow. "Excuse me?"

"Zak, are you sure?" his sister asked.

"It seems unlikely," Deevee pointed out. "Molecular alteration is an extremely complex process. It would take a computer the size of—"

"It happened," Zak replied. "I'm telling you, something is wrong here."

"Zak, how could it have changed you?" Tash said. "And how could you have changed back so quickly? Maybe you just looked at one of these crazy reflections." She reached out to one of the nearest funhouse mirrors.

"Don't touch it!" Zak yelled.

Lando frowned. "Zak, if you're that concerned, maybe we should go back to see Danna Fajji. I'm sure he can explain all this, just as he explained The Nightmare Machine."

"Oh, that makes me feel a lot better," Zak said sarcastically. But he had no better ideas, and he followed as Lando led them back toward the administrative building.

"Welcome!" Danna Fajji called out as they entered his office. He stood up from behind a curved metallic desk, where he'd been working at a computer. "I trust you found Hologram Fun World to your liking. How was The Nightmare Machine?"

"Confusing, to say the least," Lando began diplomatically. "In fact, you could say that—"

"What's going on?" Zak interrupted Lando. "First you scare me with those horror holos in The Nightmare Machine, and then something happened to me in the Hall of Reflection. What is this place?"

"The Hall of Reflection," Fajji muttered, putting his

hands together and touching his fingertips to his puffy lips. "My apologies. My hologram technicians have been experimenting with new programs. You may have discovered a glitch in the mirror room."

"A *glitch*!" Zak almost screamed.

"There, you see?" Deevee said, trying to calm Zak down. "The explanation is simple."

"I truly regret any inconvenience," Fajji insisted sincerely. "We take all complaints quite seriously, and I'll do anything I can to make your stay pleasant."

"Complaints?" Lando asked warily. "Have you gotten any other complaints? I hope they're not the kind that would concern a potential investor like me."

"Of course not! Of course not!" Fajji laughed. "In fact, I'm glad you're here, Master Calrissian. I wanted to show you some of these profit numbers . . ."

As Lando and Fajji drifted into conversation, Zak shook his head and turned away to look at the view from the window. Far off he could see the lagoon where the Whaladon swam. Closer up, Zak saw the Star Chamber, which contained a three-dimensional map of the entire galaxy. Almost beneath his feet, at the steps of the administration building, Zak could see a crowd of tourists walking across the plaza.

He wondered if he really had just been the victim of

a computer glitch. No one else seemed to be concerned about Fun World. Certainly not the crowd below him. He squinted, trying to focus on the faces of
the beings milling about the plaza.

As he did, the entire crowd vanished.

CHAPTER

Zak was so startled that he didn't cry out. He blinked, thinking his eyes were playing tricks on him.

They weren't. The plaza beneath the administration building was empty. The crowds had vanished.

"They're gone," he said in pure astonishment. "They're all just gone."

"Who's gone?" Tash asked.

"Everyone!" he said, pointing out the window.

Tash and Lando rushed to the window. As far as the eye could see, the streets were empty.

Hologram Fun World was deserted.

"See!" Zak insisted. "I told you something was going

on here." He turned to Danna Fajji and demanded, "What happened to everyone?"

Fajji stammered, "Please—please, I assure you, no one has been harmed . . ."

Lando glowered. "Zak may be right about this place after all. I think you've got some explaining to do, Fajji."

The chubby man tugged at his red beard. "Master Calrissian, I'm afraid I do owe you an explanation." He sighed. "You see, business at Hologram Fun World has not been as good lately as it could be. We haven't had many visitors. And when the park is so empty, the people that *do* come feel less excited about being here. So in order to make the park appear full, we—"

"You created holographic visitors," Tash guessed.

"Exactly," Fajji confessed. "We do have a few real visitors in Fun World, but most of the crowds you've seen today—they're computer-generated images."

"I knew it," Deevee sniffed.

"Deevee, you *knew* that?" Tash started.

"Of course," the droid replied. "Any droid worth his circuitry would know the difference."

"But most species wouldn't," Fajji acknowledged.

"An investor certainly wouldn't," Lando said accusingly. "Fajji, why do I have the feeling you were trying to trick me into investing in your Fun World?"

"Master Calrissian, I—"

"Don't say another word!" Calrissian snorted indignantly. "I'll have to reconsider our arrangement and speak to you tomorrow. Good day!"

Calrissian stomped out of Fajji's office with the two Arrandas and their droid in tow. As all four descended in the turbolift, Lando surprised his friends when his angry glare turned into a pleasant chuckle.

"Wha—?" Zak sputtered. "You're not mad? That Fajji tried to trick you, and you're laughing?"

Lando's eyes flashed mischievously. "Just a businessman's trick. I would have done the same in his place. In fact, I admire Fajji's guts for trying to pull off the hologram trick."

"But you seemed so angry in there," Zak replied.

"Remember," Lando said in return, "things are not always what they seem. Let's go back to the lodge."

That night, Zak dreamed.

He dreamed that he was on Uncle Hoole's Shi'ido homeworld—a planet that, like Uncle Hoole himself, was a mystery. At first it was calm and beautiful, with clean, well-tended streets and tall, elegant Shi'ido walking by. Zak felt peaceful and calm.

Then, in the corner of his eye, he caught a glimpse of a large head and flashing red eyes. Two long, multijointed arms wriggled through the air, reaching for him. But when Zak turned toward the image, the entire world melted and changed shape.

Suddenly he was surrounded by Imperial stormtroopers. When Zak turned to run, the world shapeshifted again, and Zak plunged into a thick bog. Swamp water rose up to his chest. As he struggled through it, Zak felt the thick tentacle of a one-eyed, water-dwelling dianoga brush past his arm.

But again his attention was caught by a movement just out of eyesight. This time Zak managed to glimpse a huge domed skull before his dream melted and changed. A whole series of nightmares blended together as Zak plunged into a pit of writhing, squirming crystal snakes.

Zak awoke suddenly. He felt the sheets crumpled around him, soaked with sweat.

Zak had had nightmares before, but never so many all at once, and never so many different kinds. It was almost as though his brain were sorting through a list of the most frightening scenes imaginable. And what was that *thing* that kept moving in the corner of his eye? He tried to recall the image exactly as it had appeared in his dream, but he couldn't.

"Just like a dream to do that," Zak muttered.

He got out of bed and went to his window. It was

morning, but still too early for anyone to be awake. All the attractions of Hologram Fun World had been shut down, and the amusement park stretched before him like a vast pool of darkness.

Zak left his room and walked down the hall to Tash's. He was surprised that Deevee wasn't standing in the hall—the caretaker droid's usual post when the two Arrandas slept. He rang Tash's door buzzer once. Then twice. On the third buzz, Zak thought he heard Tash call out from the other side of the door. He pressed the Open switch, and the door slid back.

Her room was dark, but Zak could see his sister's silhouette outlined against a view window. She was sitting on the edge of her bed, very still. Although he couldn't see her face in the dark room, he could tell she was looking at him.

"Tash," he said softly as the door slid closed behind him. "I couldn't sleep. Something about this place is still bothering me. Are you sure you aren't getting any of your . . . you know, your feelings? The Force, or whatever it is . . . isn't it telling you anything?"

His sister didn't reply.

"Tash?" he whispered. "C'mon. What's on your mind?"

Tash spoke in a slow, low voice.

"One of us must die."

"One of us must die."

Tash repeated the phrase, this time a little faster.

"Tash?" Zak replied, craning his neck forward to see her face. "What are you talking about?"

"One of us must die!" she hissed urgently.

Now that he was close enough, Zak could see that Tash's eyes were open, but her stare was blank. She was looking at him, but she seemed to see something else. It was as though she were in a deep trance.

Zak touched her shoulder, and before he could speak her name again, Tash shuddered and blinked rapidly. Her eyes closed, then opened again. This time she focused on her brother's face.

"Zak? What are you doing here?"

"What did you mean by 'one of us must die'?" he asked in return.

His sister rubbed the sleep from her eyes and brushed back a wisp of blond hair from her face. "What are you talking about?"

Zak explained how he had found Tash sitting on the edge of her bed, how she'd looked, and what she'd said.

"I don't remember saying that. I was dreaming something . . . but it's gone now. The next thing I knew, you were waking me up."

Zak told her about his own nightmares. "I just can't shake the feeling that something's wrong. Aren't you getting any of your feelings?"

Tash rubbed her forehead. "Nope. Just a headache. Sorry, Zak. Can't you try to relax? This is supposed to be our vacation. The whole point of coming to Hologram Fun World was to find a place far away from Project Starscream. Fun World may be weird, but there's nothing dangerous here."

Zak grimaced. "Don't tell me you believe what Fajji says."

Tash shrugged. "Why not? It fits, doesn't it? How could all those people vanish if they *weren't* holograms in the first place?"

70

They debated until a holographic sun rose across the artificial sky of Fun World, and Tash's door buzzer rang. Deevee entered a moment later.

"Good morning. Master Calrissian asked me to inform you both that he plans to continue to explore Fun World this morning. He's invited you both along."

Zak hesitated. He liked Lando, but he had misgivings about re-entering the park. "I don't know, Deevee . . ." he started to say.

The droid put his stiff mechanical arms on his hips. "Zak Arranda, your uncle gave me the responsibility to make sure you and your sister relaxed while at Hologram Fun World. I will not have you sulking in your room while a galaxy full of perfectly safe adventures awaits." Deevee's eyelike photoreceptors glowed at them as he waited.

Tash stood up and yawned. "C'mon, Zak. There's nothing to worry about. Let's go."

Zak found himself in a very strange position. Normally he was willing to take a chance. But even the bravest adventurer would have second thoughts after seeing himself turned into a monster in the Hall of Reflection.

Or had he?

It *could* have been a hologram, Zak told himself.

After all, that's what holograms were for—to fool people. Maybe that's all that had happened.

Besides, Zak thought, *even Deevee is encouraging me to enjoy Fun World.* Their bionic baby-sitter was normally so cautious that Zak sometimes thought he'd been programmed by a nursemaid. If he caught even a hint of danger, Deevee would have them on the next shuttle to the safest star system in a thousand light-years. Yet the droid did not fear Fun World.

"Maybe you're right," he said at last. "Let's go."

Hologram Fun World was brimming with tourists—real or holograms, Zak couldn't tell—as the Arrandas followed Deevee to their meeting place with Lando Calrissian. Lando was waiting for them in the plaza near the administration building. He looked handsome in a flowing scarlet cape that fastened around his neck with a golden cord.

"And how did you two sleep?" he asked as they approached. His sparkling eyes fell on Tash. "Are you all right? You look a bit pale."

"I've got a little headache," she said quietly. "Nothing to worry about."

Zak said, "I can't believe you're still considering getting involved in this place after everything that's gone wrong."

The gambler shrugged. "There's nothing wrong with this operation that a smooth hand couldn't fix. But I think I'll drop this 'horror' theme down a black hole. Doesn't seem to do much for the park."

A pair of Bothans happened to be walking by at that moment. "Excuse me," Zak said, stepping in front of the white-furred humanoids.

"May I be of service?" one of the Bothans asked, smoothing a tuft of hair on his cheek.

"Yes," Zak replied with just a hint of mischief, "I was just wondering. How does it feel to be an illusion?"

The Bothan's fur stiffened. "I beg your pard—"

It never finished. A powerful roar swept across the plaza like a storm, echoed by the thunder of giant footsteps crashing down on the ground.

The rancor had come back.

Screeching, the Bothans bolted for the nearest building. They dove into the administration building, and the doors slammed shut behind them.

Zak laughed. "That's prime! Those Bothans are going to feel like fools when they learn that the rancor is just a hologram."

Tash only shrugged. "Can't blame them. We did the same thing when we got here."

As they spoke, the huge rancor continued to charge

forward. Now it was ten meters away, its head lowered, its jaws open wide to swallow them.

They ignored it. "If you don't mind," Lando said casually, raising his voice to be heard over the artificial roar of the rancor, "I'd like to get your opinions on some of the other attractions. Then I'll make my final decision about Fun World."

"No problem!" Zak shouted back. "Let's just wait for this pest to pass."

"You know, an old friend once dared me to look a rancor in the eye," Lando said with a chuckle, "and I never back down from a dare." He turned and shouted right into the rancor's face. "Get outta here, meat breath! Your program couldn't fool a greenie from Circarpous IV!"

The rancor responded with lightning speed. Its massive head shot forward and its jaws snapped shut around Lando Calrissian.

CHAPTER

"Lando!" Zak cried, jumping back.

"What happened?" Tash shouted, although she and Zak both knew very well what had happened. They had both seen Lando Calrissian swallowed whole by a rancor that was *supposed* to be nothing more than an illusion.

The rancor let loose a bone-chilling roar that shook the Fun World dome. Clots of gooey red gore spilled from its open jaws.

"Run!" Deevee shrieked frantically as the rancor's tiny eyes settled on the three remaining portions of its meal.

Zak, Tash, and the droid scrambled toward the

doors to the administration building, but the portal refused to slide open.

"It's locked!" Tash cried.

"The Bothans must have locked it!" Zak guessed, pounding on the door. "Let us in!"

There was no reply, except for another triumphant roar from the rancor.

Deevee's caretaker programming took charge. "This way!" the droid ordered.

The two Arrandas followed Deevee as the droid churned his mechanical legs as fast as they would go across the plaza. The rancor hesitated a moment. Then it turned and thundered after them.

The beast had cleared the streets of real and holographic tourists alike. Zak, Tash, and Deevee were alone now as they ran from the rancor. Zak veered away and pounded on the door to the nearby Volcano Slide. That, too, was locked.

"What's going on here?" he panted, and continued running.

The rancor was gaining on them.

"Follow me," Deevee encouraged.

"Wh-Where?" Tash managed to gasp as they ran down one of Fun World's many lanes.

"To the lagoon," Deevee suggested. "The rancor will not like the water."

If the path to the lagoon had been straight, Zak and Tash would have been swallowed by the rancor's next bite. Deevee would have been crushed into scrap metal by the carnivorous beast's next footstep.

But the path wasn't straight. Zak, Tash, and Deevee made a sharp turn to the left just as the rancor pounced. Unable to turn as fast as its tiny prey, the giant predator skidded and crashed into a building, toppling a wall.

"Hurry! This is our chance!" Deevee urged.

Zak was usually faster than Tash, and much faster than the stiff-legged droid. So he was surprised to see Deevee keep ahead of him as they ran. When had the droid gotten so fast?

The persistent rancor had recovered from his crash and was gaining once again. But by now they had reached the lagoon. All three kicked up white sand as they dashed across the beach and splashed into the water.

"Get beyond its reach!" Deevee cried.

Tash and Zak waded out until the water was almost to their necks. They were a dozen meters from shore— much farther than the rancor could extend its massive claws.

The rancor rumbled across the beach, sending huge sand clouds billowing into the artificial sky. The minute its foot touched the wet sand at the water's edge, the creature stopped.

Tash rubbed water from her eyes with trembling hands. "Are you sure this will work?"

"Yes," Deevee replied as water droplets ran down his metal plating. "According to my information banks, rancors have an innate dislike for water."

The rancor growled, raised a foot, and took one mighty stomp into the ocean.

"Of course," the droid added, "I could be mistaken."

The rancor took another step. The weight of its body sent a huge wave rolling out from the shore toward them. The wave carried them farther out into the ocean.

"Great," Zak muttered. "We're still being chased, but now we can't even run."

"We may not have to worry about the rancor," Tash said gloomily. "We're being carried out to sea."

She was right. The rancor was so big that every step it took caused a huge wave. Each wave pushed the two Arrandas and the droid farther away from shore. After a few moments, Zak felt the silty floor drop away beneath his feet and he began to tread water.

Zak accidentally swallowed a mouthful of saltwater.

He gagged and shouted, "How long can you stay afloat?"

"Awhile," Tash said shakily. "But my head is killing me. I don't feel well."

"I am equipped with internal air pockets," Deevee informed Zak. "I can remain buoyant for extended periods. But my circuits will short out rather quickly in this water, I'm afraid."

"I don't think we'll be around that long," Zak groaned, pointing toward shore.

The rancor came nearer. The water had risen above its snarling jaws now, making Zak realize just how far from shore they were. All they could see were two beady black eyes and a bony ridge atop its head as it waded toward its prey.

Then it sank below the surface.

"Where is it?" Zak called out, thrashing around in the water.

"Astounding," Deevee said, weirdly calm. "It's going to strike from below."

Zak thought he felt a cold current of water rush beneath his feet, as though something large had passed through the water beneath him. He looked around frantically.

Farther out on the ocean, bubbles rose to the surface. Something was out there.

"Could it have passed us?" Tash wondered aloud.

No one had time to answer. More air bubbles burst through the surface, and then a huge gray shape rose into the air, shedding an enormous tent of water. The gray shape was at least twenty meters off, but still it loomed over the two Arrandas and their droid. Zak saw one enormous blue eye focus on him.

"The Whaladon!"

"It will give us a ride," Deevee stated.

"No kidding!" shouted Zak.

Zak began to swim, then stopped. Something else had appeared near the Whaladon. He thought he saw two flashing red eyes just beneath the water's surface. Then the salt spray made him blink, and the image was gone.

The Whaladon, meanwhile, loomed closer.

The Arrandas had ridden the Whaladon two days ago by swimming out into the lagoon, where the sea creature patiently waited as they scrambled onto its back.

This time the Whaladon did not seem to be waiting.

With a swipe of its massive tail, the giant fish shot forward—straight toward them.

Tash stopped swimming. "What's it doing?"

A line formed along the Whaladon's jaw. The line turned into an opening, and the opening grew into a gargantuan gaping mouth. The lower part of the jaw was filled with churning ocean water. The top of the jaw—ten meters above the water's surface—reached toward the sky.

"Look out!" Zak cried. But it was too late.

They were swept into the giant mouth just as the jaws snapped shut.

The Whaladon had swallowed them whole.

CHAPTER

Zak felt only water and darkness and heat and noise. For a moment he thought he had died. But when the rumbling did not stop, and the heat continued to press down on him like an enormous wet cloak, he knew that he was still alive.

Inside the Whaladon.

Zak was lying on something moist but solid, squishy but immensely strong. The spongy surface twitched, and Zak bounced into the hot, dark air, then landed with a wet splat.

I'm lying on the Whaladon's tongue, he thought. A chill of disgust ran through him.

A tiny noise reached his ears over the sounds of the Whaladon's body. He heard it again—"Zak!"—and squirmed toward the sound.

"Here!" he called into the pitch darkness.

A hand reached out and grabbed the collar of his tunic, pulling him easily along the Whaladon's slick tongue until he felt himself lying next to his sister. She was clinging to something hard and rough and pointed.

"Are you all right?" Tash shouted.

"I don't know," Zak said. "Deevee?"

"Here." Two dim round lights presented themselves. They were the glow from Deevee's photoreceptors. "We are inside the Whaladon's mouth."

Beneath them, the Whaladon's tongue surged and curled back away from the teeth. "Hold on!" Deevee said.

Zak felt a powerful force drag him backward, toward the creature's throat and stomach. He grabbed on to one of the Whaladon's teeth so hard that he felt his fingernails scrape its sides. Just as Zak felt he could hold on no longer, the tongue rolled back toward them, and Zak collapsed against the sea monster's gums.

"Hold tight," Deevee's voice warned from the darkness. "The Whaladon is sure to swallow again soon."

"I can't stand it!" Tash shouted. There was panic in her voice, the same terror Zak felt swelling in his own chest. "Why didn't it just swallow us and finish this?"

"Tash!" Zak yelled. "Don't give up! We've got to find a way out of here!"

"Why?" she said in despair. "What's the use? Things will only get worse."

Zak was worried. It wasn't like Tash to give up. Despite the thick heat, the darkness, and the droning sound of the Whaladon's body and lungs, Zak tried to calm his own fear and think clearly.

"Don't think that way, Tash," he began. "You can't."

"What difference does it make?" she said weakly.

"It makes a difference to me!" he argued. "C'mon, Tash! You're all I have left. And I'm all you have left. We've always helped one another. You can't quit now!"

"Watch out!" Deevee called.

Once again, the massive tongue rolled back. Zak hugged the hard, slippery tooth to keep from being pulled down the monster's throat. Beside him he heard Tash sob. Then she cried out. Then she was gone.

"Tash!" Zak yelled. "Are you there?"

No answer.

"Tash!"

Under the roar of the Whaladon's noisy innards,

Zak heard a faint moan. Tash had lost her grip on the Whaladon tooth and was lying somewhere on the monster's huge tongue. When the Whaladon swallowed again, she would be lost forever.

Zak did not want to give up his secure hold. But he did not want to lose his sister either. Releasing his grip, Zak let himself slide blindly back along the giant, wriggling tongue. He thrashed his arms about until one hand brushed along Tash's jacket, and he grabbed hold. Tash let out a short cry as they both slid another meter, then stopped.

"Come on!" he ordered. He got to his knees and, still holding Tash's jacket, pulled her back toward what he thought was the front of the Whaladon's mouth. Finally his free hand touched something hard, and he clung to the Whaladon's tooth.

"Now," he gasped, "we've got to get out of here."

"I believe I can help."

As Zak and Tash turned toward Deevee's voice, the droid was suddenly illuminated by the glow of a small laser torch. Its orange light reflected off the water drops dripping down Deevee's wet metallic body.

"Where did you get that?" Zak asked.

"I equipped myself with a laser torch recently to effect personal repairs," the droid replied. "It seems to have been a fortunate addition."

"Why didn't you tell us before?" Tash snapped.

Deevee 'explained, "It would not have done any good. The Whaladon had submerged. We would have escaped its mouth only to drown in deep water. But my sensors tell me the creature has surfaced again. Brace yourselves."

In the light of the torch, Zak and Tash watched Deevee aim the cutting tool toward the roof of the Whaladon's cavernous mouth and press the trigger. A thin beam of superheated energy shot through the murky air and punctured the top of the creature's mouth.

A deep, roaring sound of distress rolled through the cavern. The tongue slapped upward, nearly tearing Tash and Zak from their perch, then slammed downward onto the base of the giant mouth. Warm, slimy saliva splashed over their bodies.

The Whaladon bellowed.

Deevee fired again, and the creature shook once more. This time, it let out a low-pitched moan and opened its wounded mouth. Sunlight and saltwater sprayed into the cavern in a rush of wind. Over the white foam, Zak saw the clear blue waters of the holographic ocean.

"Jump to the side!" Deevee yelled.

Zak and Tash pulled themselves atop the massive

tooth and jumped into the water to one side of the Whaladon. Deevee jumped to the other side just as the mighty jaws closed again.

The roar of rushing water filled Zak's ears, and the cold sea covered him. Holding his breath, he tumbled underwater for a few panicked seconds in the Whaladon's wake, not knowing which way was up or down. He tried to calm himself, and relaxed, knowing that gravity would tell him where to go. His lungs started to burn from lack of oxygen. After a moment, he felt himself bob upward, and he kicked in that direction.

Zak's head broke the surface and he gasped, filling his lungs with air. He wiped saltwater from his eyes. He floated on the ocean's surface, bobbing wildly in the wake of the sea monster. In moments, the fast-moving Whaladon was little more than a gray lump on the horizon.

"Tash! Deevee!" he called out. No one replied, but Zak saw a patch of blondish hair fly up over the swelling water and he swam for it. He reached his sister, who gasped and coughed out saltwater. Her eyes were half-open but dazed.

There was no sign of Deevee.

He can't drown, Zak thought to himself. *Maybe he got pulled along by the current.*

Tash would soon sink if she didn't snap out of it. Using one hand to keep her afloat, Zak started to swim toward the shore.

Zak had done plenty of swimming on Alderaan. He swam steadily but slowly, to save his strength, and after fifteen minutes they were near enough to see the shoreline clearly. There was no sign of the rancor.

Exhausted and soaking wet, Zak crawled onto the wet sand, hauling his sister behind him. "I've never swum so far in my whole life," he panted.

Beside him Tash let out a huge gasp. Still only half-conscious, she muttered, "One of us must die. One of us must die . . ."

Zak grabbed her shoulders. "Tash? What are you saying?"

Tash let out a sudden, violent cough, clearing more water from her lungs. Her eyes flew open. "Zak!" She looked around. "We're—we're on dry land!"

"Yeah," he sighed wearily. "What were you saying just now? You were muttering again. Are you sick?"

"I don't know." She rubbed her temples. "I don't remember saying anything. But my head is killing me. What did I say?"

Zak decided not to tell her. "Forget it. You were just delirious."

Tash shivered in her wet clothes.

"We've got to find help," Zak said. "We've got to find out what's going on here. How could that rancor have *eaten* Lando? Wasn't it a hologram?"

Tash didn't answer. She still seemed lost in her own world.

Zak answered his own question. "I don't know. I told you something's wrong here. It's like the Hall of Reflection. I really felt like I had been transformed, not just tricked by an illusion." He pointed to the nearest building, a long, low structure at the edge of the lagoon. "Whatever that rancor is, I don't want it to find us. Let's stay out of the open. We should head for that building over there."

Slowly Tash and Zak made their way toward a building surrounded by small kiosks. The kiosks contained arts and crafts from across the galaxy—woven baskets spun from the grass fields of Worru'du, magnificent animated storytelling puppets from the planet Zhann, and delicate figurines made from seashells on the many-tiered world of K'ath.

The objects in the kiosks were beautiful, but all Zak and Tash noticed was that all the people were gone.

"Maybe they were all holograms," Tash offered

hopefully. "Maybe they were just accidentally erased, like the other day."

"Or maybe," Zak returned darkly, "they were real. Maybe everything is real now. Otherwise how could that rancor have eaten Lando?" He swallowed. "Everything in Fun World has come to life."

The building beyond the kiosks was topped by a sign that read, THE MAKER'S WORKSHOP.

"Do you think this place is safe?" Tash asked.

"I don't know," her brother answered. "But it can't be worse than anyplace else in Fun World. Besides, maybe we'll find Deevee here. It sounds like the kind of place a droid would like."

Inside The Maker's Workshop, they found a long hall. On each side of the hall was a workbench, and another long table ran down the middle of the room.

"Prime!" Zak exclaimed when he saw the tables.

The tables, shelves, and even parts of the floor were covered with mechanical parts and tools. Servos, circuits, hydrospanners, the arms and legs and heads of disassembled droids, even engine parts, lay scattered everywhere. It was a tinkerer's paradise.

"Imagine what I could do with all this stuff," he murmured to himself. He walked down one row of parts. "There's enough spare equipment in this room to build a dozen droids, a T-71 skyhopper—maybe even a small starship!"

"Don't get any ideas, Zak," Tash warned. "This isn't the time to—"

She stopped. In the middle of the central table, resting on a small pedestal of polished stone, was a gleaming cylinder that Tash recognized instantly. It was the weapon of a Jedi Knight.

It was a lightsaber.

Tash had only seen one lightsaber before with her own eyes. It had been worn on the hip of a young man named Luke Skywalker who, along with his friends, had saved them from the flesh-eating planet D'vouran.

Tash exhaled slowly. A lightsaber. Only the Jedi knew how to build them. Only the Jedi knew how to use them properly. Where had it come from? How had it gotten here?

It's probably just a hologram, she thought. But then, the rancor was supposed to be a hologram, wasn't it? Maybe the lightsaber would prove to be just as real.

With a lightsaber, Tash felt she would be one step closer to becoming a Jedi Knight. With one of those powerful laser swords in her hand, there was nothing she couldn't do. She could be a hero.

Nearby, Zak stood before a table full of droid parts,

his eyes jumping from one piece to another. In his mind he had already designed his own hyperdrive, built a personal droid with antigravity repulsors and long-range sensors for detecting angry adults, and a stream-lined skimboard that could go vertical and climb the sides of even the highest buildings.

But Zak found the biggest prize of all a few meters down the line. Sitting under a bright light was a droid head, but not just any droid head.

"A BT-2000," Zak whistled under his breath. "That's the most advanced droidwork in the galaxy. The computer brain in that droid could run all the functions on a Star Destroyer. I'd love to see what makes it tick."

Zak reached out his hands and picked up the droid head.

Tash reached out and picked up the lightsaber.

Before Zak, the droid's photoreceptors blazed with light. The head swiveled in his hands, and a booming voice exploded from the mouthspeaker.

"WHO DISTURBS THE MAKER'S SLEEP?"

Zak stumbled back in shock, dropping the head. Startled by her brother, Tash instinctively pressed the lightsaber's activation switch. It burst into fire and light.

The droid's burning eyes continued to glare at Zak.

"THE CRAFT OF THE MAKER IS FORBIDDEN TO THE LIVING! INTRUDERS, PREPARE TO MEET YOUR DOOM!"

The light in the droid's eyes faded. For a moment, the room was silent except for the hiss of the lightsaber in Tash's hand.

Then every object in the workshop came to life. Gears whirred and gyros spun as dozens of machines turned to face Zak.

Then they attacked.

CHAPTER 13

The Maker's Workshop had turned into a hurricane of flying metal parts and electronic wires. Cogwheels collided with hydropistons; mechanical arms attached themselves to wheels. Zak saw two droid arms without bodies fuse themselves to a pair of tractor treads and start rolling toward Zak and Tash.

"This is impossible," he said out loud. "Impossible!" *Gadgets could not put themselves together!* he wanted to shout. *Machines did not turn themselves on. Technology would not turn on living beings!*

He jumped out of the way as the mechanical droid arms clutched at him. But dodging the arms only put him within reach of a hydrospanner that had come to life and was boring its way toward his forehead. He ducked, and the hydrospanner buried itself in the wall.

All around him, ragtag pieces of metal, odds and ends of junk, were combining to form misshapen mechanical monsters with wires for hair, glow rods for eyes, and multiple arms made of whatever material lay at hand.

"This can't be happening!" Zak shouted.

"But it is," said a gravelly voice. Zak saw the droid head still resting on the table. Its eyes were once more lit up and glaring at Zak. "You are the little tinkerer," the droid spoke. "You like to experiment with technology. You like to take things apart. How do you feel now that technology is going to take *you* apart? Destroy him!"

Zak was so terrified he couldn't move. This was worse than a nightmare—it was a fear that he did not even know he had, something buried deep in his brain. He was terrified, and he could only think of one thing. Where was Tash?

Tash was paralyzed, too. She saw the mechanical junk come to life. She heard the droid head threaten Zak. She felt the lightsaber quivering in her hand, waiting to be used.

But she couldn't move.

95

Here was her chance to prove her Jedi potential. All she had to do was charge into the crowd of whirling machines and robots, cutting through them with her unstoppable lightsaber. She could save her brother using a Jedi weapon. She could *be* a Jedi.

But what if I fail?

The thought froze her muscles. What if she found out, after all this time, that she really didn't have the Force? That she couldn't use a lightsaber? That all her hopes and dreams were just a fantasy?

She was terrified.

"Tash! Help!" Zak called. The machines were closing in. Most had attached tools to the ends of their mechanical arms. As they came closer, needles, blades, and saws began to whir.

"Tash!" Zak repeated. His back was to the wall. He was trapped. "Use the lightsaber!"

Tash could not do it. She wanted to be a Jedi Knight more than anything else in the galaxy. But she was afraid to fail.

"I'm—I'm sorry, Zak," she whispered.

She deactivated the lightsaber and dropped it to the floor.

"Tash!" Zak groaned.

But to the surprise of both Arrandas, the moment Tash shut down the energy blade, all the machines stopped. They fell apart in cascades of metal scraps. In seconds, the floor was once more littered with lifeless junk.

Zak gaped at the semicircle of harmless scrap at his feet. "How did you do that?" he asked.

"I didn't do anything," his sister said, nearly in tears.

Zak didn't waste any time. "Well, whatever. It worked. Let's get out of here."

They hurried out of The Maker's Workshop and into the empty streets of Hologram Fun World. There was still no one in sight.

"Maybe we should get out of here," Zak suggested. "We should find Deevee. Find someplace where the holograms aren't working."

"You're the technobrain," his sister replied wearily. "Where would that be?"

Zak considered. "The airlock. We didn't see any holograms until we left the airlock. Let's go."

They hurried in the direction of the space dock and its airlock. Now and then they heard the rancor roar down some distant street. Each time, they froze in their tracks and waited until its ground-shaking footsteps faded away.

Tash had been silent. Zak looked over at her. She was muttering something under her breath.

". . . one of us must die . . . one of us must die . . ." she breathed.

"Tash!" Zak yelled. He shook her shoulders. "Quit it! What does that mean?"

Tash blinked and her eyes focused on him. "Wh-What?"

"You said it again. 'One of us must die.' What does that mean?"

His sister shook her head. "I'm sorry, Zak. I don't know. I don't even know I'm doing it. It must be important, but I just don't know."

"All right, just forget it. Look, here's the airlock."

They had arrived at a heavy steel portal set in the massive dome. Beyond the door was a room that led to another door. And that door led to the space dock.

"We'll just wait in the airlock for now, until we can figure out what to do. The holograms won't work there," said Zak.

"Okay," Tash said, reaching to press the switch that activated the automatic door.

Zak was distracted by a movement in the other direction. Four spidery limbs crawled into his line of sight. This time he whipped his head around and caught full sight of the brain creature. Its long arms and legs clung to the side of the space dome as its enormous head bobbed back and forth, red eyes burning bright. Two flailing tentacles flapped out of its open mouth. It looked bigger.

"Tash, wait!" Zak warned.

Too late. The door opened. For a fraction of a second, Zak and Tash were able to look out the door—a door that opened into the icy-cold vacuum of space.

Then Tash was sucked out into the void.

CHAPTER 14

Zak just barely managed to grab Tash's arm before she was pulled into deep space. Air from inside the dome began rushing out into empty space, dragging Tash and Zak along with it. Zak held Tash with one hand and clung to the edge of the doorway with the other. He had seen deep space and stars before, of course, but always from the safety of a starship viewport. Now he was looking at the eternal night with his naked eye. He didn't like it.

"Pull me back!" Tash gasped over the rushing wind.

"I can't!" he said, gritting his teeth. "Pull yourself!"

Tash tried to use Zak's arm as a rope to pull herself

back into Fun World. But the escaping air dragged at her face and clothes.

"I can't!" she yelled.

"You have to!" Zak demanded. He had already lost his parents and friends. His uncle was away, and now even Deevee was gone. He could not lose his only sister, the only *family* he had left. "Try!"

Tash gritted her teeth. Hand over hand, she pulled herself to safety. Centimeter by centimeter, she fought the wind that sucked her into space, until she was back inside the dome. Zak slapped the Close switch. The minute the heavy door slid back into place, the powerful suction force stopped, and Tash collapsed to the ground.

For a moment the two Arrandas lay next to each other, gasping for breath.

"Wh-What is this place?" Tash nearly sobbed. "It's like a giant death trap."

"I don't know," Zak panted. "Everything's wrong here. I don't know why this is happening."

"I do."

Standing before them was Uncle Hoole! Both Arrandas got to their feet and threw their arms around him with relief. Hoole returned their hugs awkwardly. The stern expression never left his face.

"Uncle Hoole, we've got to get out of here," Zak

explained in one hurried breath. "The holograms are alive and they're killing people. They killed Lando, a gambler we met, and Deevee's missing. And The Nightmare Machine creature is lurking about, I don't know what it is, but we've got to—"

"Remain calm," Hoole said steadily. "I have already discovered the cause of the occurrences. I assure you, everything is under control. Now follow me."

Zak and Tash were so relieved to see their uncle, so calm and in control, that they followed him willingly. This time when Zak spied a movement out of the corner of his eye, he ignored it. Whatever the creature from The Nightmare Machine was, Hoole would deal with it.

But the Shi'ido led them straight to the administration building at the heart of Hologram Fun World.

"Wait!" Zak almost shouted. "We can't go back there!"

Hoole didn't even pause. "The answers to your questions are within."

Tash and Zak looked at one another. They had no choice but to follow their uncle.

Like the rest of Fun World, the administration building seemed deserted. The silence made Zak even more nervous. Alone, the three rode a turbolift to the top of the building and entered Danna Fajji's office. The baron administrator sat at his desk with his hands folded neatly in his lap.

"Welcome, welcome," Fajji said. "I understand you've had quite a day here at Hologram Fun World."

"Quite a day!" Tash snapped. "Your holograms killed our friend! They almost killed us!"

Fajji chuckled. "Oh, no, no, no. I assure you no one has been killed. At least, not yet."

With startling quickness, the smile fell away from Fajji's face.

Then Fajji's face itself fell away.

The baron administrator's skin crawled across his frame, and in two blinks of an eye he had changed shape.

Tash and Zak were looking at another Shi'ido.

"Gog!" Zak cried. But the presence of the evil scientist was not nearly as terrifying as what happened next. Gog turned to Uncle Hoole and nodded satisfactorily. "Excellent work, Dr. Hoole."

Hoole shrugged. "It was quite simple. They are trusting."

"You can't be working with him!" Tash insisted in a panic. "He's your enemy."

"He's *your* enemy," Hoole replied. "Gog and I have been working together since the beginning of Project Starscream."

Zak shook his head. "It can't be true!"

"It is," Gog said. "And now we'll prove it. Hoole, destroy these two interlopers."

A blaster appeared in Uncle Hoole's hand. He put it right between Zak's eyes.

CHAPTER

Zak felt the cold metal of the blaster press against his forehead and braced himself for the shot.

Hoole did not fire right away. He waited, prolonging the moment of terror with an evil laugh. A quiver of terror ran through Zak like a groundquake, and he hugged himself to keep still.

His hand brushed against something hard in the pocket of his tunic.

He felt the square shape of the sabacc card shuffler and pulled it out.

"Enough torment, Hoole," Gog said. "End this once and for all."

Hoole nodded and began to squeeze the trigger. But

before he did, Zak shoved the sabacc shuffler in Hoole's face and squeezed. The sabacc cards rattled and flew out of the shuffler chute. A deck full of hard plastic wafers slapped Hoole in the face. The Shi'ido grunted and reeled backward, waving his free hand before him to clear his sight.

"Run!" Zak yelled.

Tash was already ahead of him, racing for the turbolift. Zak slipped into the lift just as the doors closed.

"Everything's gone crazy! Everything!" he shouted at the walls.

Tash's only answer was a violent shudder and a whisper: "One of us must die."

The lift doors opened and they ran for the exit. As they reached it, they heard another turbolift open, and a blaster shot burned a hole in the wall to their left. Hoole was chasing them.

They were running through a horror-filled amusement park, being chased by their own uncle, who was working for the galaxy's most evil scientist. Zak realized that Tash might be right—they might not get out of Fun World alive.

A blaster bolt passed so close to Zak, he heard it burn the air around his ear.

"In here!" he panted, and ducked into the nearest doorway.

He stumbled forward and found himself floating in deep space.

This time, however, it was not the lifeless cold of real space. Zak was standing in the cavernous Star Chamber, which he and Tash had visited on their first day in Hologram Fun World. Stars and planets whirled past his head.

"Zak? You okay?" Tash said weakly. He saw her in the light of a passing sun, nine planets spinning around it.

"I feel like you sound," he answered.

"I'm miserable," she replied. "This is worse than anything, Zak. I thought it hurt when Mom and Dad died, but this . . ." she choked on the rest of her words. "And I failed. I could have saved you from those machines. I could have used the lightsaber. But I blew it. I want to be a Jedi so badly, but I was always afraid to fail . . ."

"You didn't blow it, Tash," Zak said. "I think you saved us by dropping the lightsaber. It didn't matter that you were afraid."

Something about his own words pricked Zak's memory, but before he could follow the thought, a new solar system came rushing through the void at them.

"Zak!" Tash started. "Do you know what system that is?"

"You're the one who does all the studying."

"It's Alderaan!"

She was right. He recognized the planets of the Alderaan system—including the hologram of their own blue-green planet. The system swept toward them and then slowed down, hovering a few meters away.

Zak swallowed. "I never thought I'd see home again, even in a hologram."

Then a single sphere appeared in the darkness. It was silver, and cold, and as it approached, they saw the thousands of laser towers on its surface. The approaching globe was pocked by one single indentation, like an eye, that slowly rotated toward the planet Alderaan.

It was the Death Star.

"No!" Zak and Tash yelled together.

The Death Star's eye began to glow as the massive battle station powered up its superlaser. There was a blinding flash. A powerful energy beam streaked through the holographic darkness and punctured Alderaan. A second later, nothing remained of the planet but a cloud of debris spreading out through space.

Tash and Zak's despair turned to fear when the Death Star rotated to face them.

"I've got a bad feeling about this," Zak warned, backpedaling away. "Where's the door?"

Tash scanned the room, but saw only the whirling planets of the galaxy. "I don't see it."

"Here!" a voice called out.

Tash and Zak recognized the sound immediately. "Deevee!"

"Over here!" the droid called again.

They ran toward the sound, dodging in and out of a dozen star systems, running from one end of the galaxy to the other, outrunning even the holographic Death Star.

Deevee stood in a square of light framed by the doorway, holding out one beckoning hand. Sprinting past him, they burst out of the galaxy and back into Fun World.

"Thank goodness I found you!" Deevee started. "I've been all over this holographic madhouse—"

"Never mind that!" Zak snapped. "We need a place to hide. This entire place is a killing machine. And I think Uncle Hoole is involved."

The droid's circuits whirred. "Master Hoole? You must be mistaken—"

His sentence was cut off by a blaster bolt that sizzled through the space between the droid and the boy. Hoole had found them.

"This way!" the droid said. "I know where we can hide."

Zak and Tash followed their caretaker droid, who hurried down a few twisting, turning lanes past the Volcano Slide and the Hall of Reflection.

Although Hoole was out of sight in a few moments, Deevee kept up the pace. Tash, however, could go no farther. "My head—I have to rest," she said. She staggered over to a small stone bench and sat down.

"We can't stop!" Deevee cried.

"No," Zak replied. "We can't go any farther now anyway."

"It's not safe here!" Deevee nearly screeched.

"It's too much, Deevee," Tash gasped, trying to clear her head. "Everything that's happened. It's like our worst nightmares come true."

His sister's words struck Zak like a blow to the head. *It's like our worst nightmares come true.*

"Tash, that's it!"

Everything came into focus like a steamed mirror suddenly clearing. "That's why we keep stumbling across all these terrible scenes. That's how the rancor killed Lando. And why I was attacked by technology. And why you blew your chance to be a Jedi."

Tash didn't understand. "Zak, what are you—"

Zak interrupted his sister. "Yes! That's why Uncle Hoole betrayed us—because you and I have both been afraid that the one adult willing to take us in might turn out to be evil. And we were both forced to con-front our worst fear—the destruction of Alderaan!" He looked at his sister. "We've gone through our worst nightmares because it's part of the program.

"We're still inside The Nightmare Machine!"

CHAPTER 16

"Nonsense," Deevee said flatly.

Tash blinked. "We left The Nightmare Machine, remember, Zak? We haven't been inside it since yesterday."

"Exactly," the droid added.

"Exactly *wrong*," Zak almost shouted. "We never left. Everything that has happened since then has happened inside The Nightmare Machine. Remember that creature I saw the first time I went in? It's the same one I've been seeing ever since. Fajji said that the program read people's minds to discover their fears. But Deevee said that no machine could read minds—only certain living beings."

Deevee admitted, "Actually, Zak, on further consideration, I think I may have erred. It might be possible—"

"Besides," Tash interjected, "Fajji said they'd invented new technology."

"He was lying!" her brother insisted. "That brain creature must read minds and create the illusions. I really did see it. And we both just saw Gog. If Gog's here now, that means he could have been here before—and I could have actually seen him experimenting on those two kids! We're in big trouble here!"

He leaped to his feet. "We've got to get back to The Nightmare Machine. That's the only way out."

"That wouldn't be wise," Deevee quickly countered. "We should stay here."

Zak furrowed his brow. "A minute ago you wanted us to find a hiding place. Now you want us to stay here?"

To Tash, Zak's argument sounded unbelievable. She was willing to believe that hidden machines created the illusion of a rancor or another person next to her—but what machine could make her think an entire space station like Fun World was real, and keep up the illusion for two days? "Zak, if Gog were behind this, why wouldn't he have just killed us? He's had the chance."

"I don't know," her brother said. "Maybe he's testing out The Nightmare Machine creature. Think about it. It's the *fear* we were put through, never the real danger. Every time we were about to actually get killed, we were saved by—" Zak stopped cold. He looked at Deevee. "We were saved by you."

The droid stiffened indignantly. "I was merely doing my duty."

Zak did not respond at first. He could not. He remembered how fast Deevee had run from the rancor. How Deevee had suddenly produced a laser torch to open the Whaladon's mouth. How Deevee had appeared just as the Death Star was about to disintegrate them.

"You've been reacting to the holograms," Zak said, his voice barely above a whisper.

"What?" Tash asked.

"Deevee's been reacting to the holograms. The rancor. The Whaladon. The Death Star. He's been treating them like they're real. But he said he couldn't do that, remember?"

The droid huffed. "Zak Arranda, I was merely doing my duty as your caretaker, as I have in the past."

"If your opponent's acting normal under unusual circumstances, you can bet he's bluffing," Zak recited Lando's lesson.

He looked at his sister. "Tash. Deevee is a hologram, too."

As the words left Zak's mouth, Deevee emitted a roar of supreme rage. His body began to change. Small hatches opened up in his metal plating, producing laser weapons and vibroblades. His face changed into a gruesome metallic war mask.

Deevee had transformed into a battle droid.

Zak stumbled backward and tripped over the stone bench, barely dodging a slashing vibroblade as Tash scrambled out of the way. The battle droid that had once been Deevee hesitated a moment, unsure which target to pursue. Seeing his chance, Zak broke into a run, circling around the droid and joining up with his sister. Together they ran.

"D-Do we need to run?" Tash gasped. "I mean, if it's just a hologram . . ."

"Ask Lando," Zak sputtered in reply. "Whatever's happening here, it's real enough to kill if we let it. We have to find a way out. We have to get back to The Nightmare Machine."

Zak turned down a street he thought led back toward the center of Fun World. But the nightmarish landscape had fooled him. Instead of heading toward The Nightmare Machine, Zak and Tash found themselves on the green gem path they'd followed when they first arrived at Hologram Fun World. Before they knew it, they were standing at the door to the airlock.

"Blaster shot!" Zak swore. "How do we get back to The Nightmare Machine?"

"If we're already inside The Nightmare Machine, I'm not sure that would help, or that we could," Tash guessed. "How did Fajji say to end the game?"

"Of course!" Zak said. He yelled at the top of his lungs, "End simulation!"

Nothing happened.

He yelled it again and again. Each time nothing happened—except that his voice drew the battle droid to them. The droid appeared at the far end of the path, stomping toward them.

"It's not working," Zak groaned.

"What's the other way?" Tash tried to think. "Fajji said there was another way."

Zak remembered. "To win the game, you have to face your worst fear. Maybe that's what we have to do!"

"But we already have! We've lost our uncle! We lost Deevee! I lost the power I thought was the Force! What more could happen?"

Zak knew. He knew it as surely as he knew his own name, and he said it quickly. "We could lose each other."

The battle droid was closing in on them. "My *worst* fear isn't being attacked by technology, or eaten by a rancor, or even losing Uncle Hoole. Tash, my worst fear is losing you! My sister!"

The battle droid was almost upon them.

"Don't you see? We haven't faced our worst fear yet because we're still together!"

Zak's urgent words cut through Tash's brain like a laser. In the time it took to think a thought, she realized: "My intuition. It has been working all along. It's been trying to tell me, Zak. 'One of us must die!' Get it?"

A blaster bolt melted the gems in the path at their feet.

Zak looked around, and his eye settled on the airlock door. He pushed open the first door, and stepped into the airtight room beyond. Now just one thick door separated him from the lifeless void. He pointed. "Should we go together?"

Tash shook her head. "I think we have to separate. That's the fear. Being apart. *Losing* each other."

He nodded and reached for the button that would open the second door. "Zak!" Tash burst out. "Listen, I tease you a lot, but you're my brother, and—"

"Yeah," he said, happy to interrupt his sister for once in a conversation. "Me too."

Zak put his hand on the button and looked back. The battle droid was almost in reach of Tash. At the last moment, he hesitated. A new fear chilled his heart. What if *Tash* were a hologram, too? What if she were an illusion designed to trick him into destroying himself?

He shrugged. That was just another fear he was going to have to face.

He pushed the button.

Zak felt like the hands of an invisible giant had thrown him out of Fun World. Head over heels, he found himself spinning out into . . . nothing. It wasn't air, it wasn't water. It was the void, and it was so cold that his bones turned instantly brittle.

Everything went black.

CHAPTER

Zak woke with a jolt, as though his mind had suddenly slammed back into his body. He was lying on cold metal. For a moment, he could not move. His body felt heavy. His arms and legs were numb. He felt like he'd been sleeping for many hours. He could not open his eyes.

Straining with his ears, Zak heard a soft, wet, squishing sound, like the sound of liquid passing through a suction tube. The sound was very close. He listened carefully.

The sound was coming from right between his own eyes.

Because he was blind, his other senses sharpened, and Zak felt the skin on his forehead.

Something was stuck to the skin of his head. Something was stuck *into* the skin of his head.

Gathering all his strength, Zak forced his eyes to open. He was staring into a bright light and he blinked once, twice, three times, before his vision cleared.

He was lying down, looking up at the ceiling of The Nightmare Machine.

Between him and the ceiling, on a pedestal, crouched the brain creature. It screeched angrily at him. Zak managed to sit up.

Tash was lying on a table next to him, and she, too, was waking up. Beyond her was another table, and still another, where other victims lay unconscious. Each of them had a thick, wet tentacle attached to their foreheads. The strings of flesh stretched from each victim back to the fearsome creature's gaping mouth.

Zak's stomach turned when he realized that he, too, had a tentacle attached to his head. Gagging, he grabbed at the tendril. It ripped away from his skin with a sickening squish, and The Nightmare Machine creature wailed. Beside him, Tash freed herself the same way.

The creature squealed in pain and rose up to its full height. Its weird spindly arms thrashed through the air.

Then it fell back into a quivering crouch, snarling at Zak and Tash.

Zak and Tash backed away from the creature. The monster took one menacing step off its pedestal.

Zak felt his back touch a wall, and at the same time, he realized someone on the other side was pounding desperately on it. He turned, saw a door, and quickly slapped the opener. The door slid back.

Lando Calrissian leaped into the room, a small hold-out blaster in his hand. The brain creature took another step forward, snarling at the newcomer. Without hesitating, Lando leveled his weapon and fired. An energy bolt pierced the creature's oversized head, shattering its skull.

"Lando!" Zak cried joyfully. "You're alive!"

The gambler's roguish grin was gone. "I could say the same for you, kid." He looked back over his shoulder. "Don't count your dragon eggs before they're hatched. We're not out of this yet."

"I'm afraid Master Calrissian is correct," said a familiar voice. Deevee stepped into the room. The *real* Deevee, Zak knew. He did not bother to greet his two charges. "The stormtroopers are closing in."

"Stormtroopers?" Tash asked.

Lando explained in a rush. "When you and Zak went back into The Nightmare Machine, Deevee and I were locked out. I complained to Fajji, but he said it was simply a malfunction. He said you were safe, and the problem would be corrected shortly. Deevee and I decided not to wait. You had already been in here an hour. We tried to break into the building a few minutes ago, and a squad of stormtroopers appeared out of nowhere!"

"Wait a minute!" Zak sputtered. "We've only been in here an hour? It seemed like days!"

"*Days*?" Lando asked. An energy beam shattered the wall beside him. "Never mind!"

"SURRENDER OR BE DESTROYED!" The voice that boomed over a loudspeaker was too powerful to be ignored. Zak peeked over Lando's shoulder as the gambler poked his head out of the building.

A hundred stormtroopers aimed their blasters at him.

They had no choice but to surrender. Lando dropped his blaster and stepped out into the open, followed by Zak, Tash, and Deevee. Stormtroopers rushed forward, roughly searching them all for any hidden weapons. Then they slapped binders on each of their wrists, including Deevee's. When the prisoners were secure, the crowd of stormtroopers parted, and a tall, gray, scowling figure stepped forward.

Borborygmus Gog.

The evil Shi'ido stepped past them and peered inside The Nightmare Machine. When he returned, his scowl had deepened into seething anger.

"You," he began, his voice filled with rage. "You two pathetic human children have caused me more trouble than a dozen rebellious star systems. You have destroyed every stage of Project Starscream, and now you have destroyed my latest experiment!" He pointed at the building. "The Nightmare Machine was a masterpiece of genetic mutation. A creature capable of entering into its victims' nightmares, and using their own fears against them."

"You were using Fun World as an experiment," Zak said.

"You were using it on us!" Tash added. "But we figured you out."

The Shi'ido's eyes narrowed. "Indeed. You two are most remarkable." His dark eyes focused on Zak. "You are quite a resourceful young man, and you"—he glared at Tash—"this intuition of yours is intriguing. The Force, perhaps? We shall see."

Gog snapped his fingers, and the stormtroopers came to attention. "Guards. Take them all back to my starship. I want them transported to my laboratory. I plan to perform some in-depth experiments."

The way Gog said the word "experiments" made Zak's blood run cold.

Stormtroopers grabbed their arms and dragged them to a nearby hovercar. The four prisoners were loaded into the car. One stormtrooper took the driver's seat while the other stood guard over the captives. The hovercar hummed away from The Nightmare Machine.

No one spoke as the hovercar carried them to a nearby airlock. The guarding stormtrooper grabbed the prisoners one by one and hauled them through the airlock and into a waiting shuttle craft.

Inside the shuttle craft, Zak and the others sat in the cargo area behind the two pilot seats. A black-uniformed Imperial pilot sat in one seat. The guarding stormtrooper took the other.

A moment later, the shuttle detached itself from Fun World. From the back of the shuttle, Zak could just see the darkness of space through the front viewport. He watched as a tiny pinpoint of light grew into a massive star cruiser.

Zak looked at his sister and whispered, "Tash, I—"

"Quiet!" the black-garbed pilot snapped. He looked at the stormtrooper. "If they speak one more word, turn them all into Sarkanian jelly."

The stormtrooper nodded and raised his blaster threateningly.

Then he smashed the weapon against the side of the pilot's head.

The pilot collapsed to the floor, unconscious.

"What in the galaxy—?" Lando gasped.

He was staring at the stormtrooper who was shimmering and twisting spasmodically.

When the stormtrooper stopped moving, Zak and Tash could not believe their eyes—the stormtrooper was Hoole!

Zak was the first to recover. "Uncle Hoole, how did you find us?"

"Time is short, Zak," the Shi'ido said tersely. "Let us say my investigation proved successful. I learned that Gog had come here. I raced to Fun World as soon as I could. Thanks to the distraction created by this gentle"—he pointed at Lando—"and Deevee, I was able to disguise myself as a stormtrooper and infiltrate Gog's army."

Lando shook his head. "I've seen some pretty weird stuff in the galaxy," he murmured, "but this wins the prize. "

Hoole did not respond. With Lando's help, he quickly tied the unconscious pilot to a passenger seat, then turned to the ship's instruments and the shuttle roared into full power. The ship swerved off course and blasted away from Hologram Fun World and the waiting cruiser.

Aboard the starship, Gog's henchmen were startled to see their master's shuttle change course. But by the time they had turned their ship to pursue, the shuttle was gone.

EPILOGUE

Hours later, Gog's shuttle had been abandoned to the depths of space. Lando had summoned his own ship using his remote control device, and his space yacht now hovered next to the *Shroud.*

Over the comm system, Lando spoke. "Isn't there any way I can help you?"

"We could not ask it of you," Hoole replied. "You will be safest if you keep your distance. I fear we have made a powerful enemy."

There was a pause, then Lando's voice came back. "I know where you can hide. I'm on my way to investigate a Tibanna gas mine on Bespin. You'll be safe there."

Again, Hoole refused. Zak spoke into the microphone. "Thanks for everything, Lando, and good luck!"

Lando laughed. "And you remember, Zak, that luck's got nothing to do with it!"

Long after Lando's space yacht had roared away, Hoole listened solemnly as Zak and Tash told them about their nightmare trip to Fun World and about the strange creature Gog had created.

When they were done, Hoole closed his eyes briefly and whispered to himself. "It is worse than I feared. Gog is farther along than I suspected."

Zak cocked his head. "Did you know about The Nightmare Machine experiment?"

Hoole shook his head. "No. I've known very little about Gog's experiments until recently. After I left you two at Hologram Fun World, I called on some . . . private sources. I learned that Gog's next experiment involved that creature. I also learned that he had discovered your location and was planning his revenge. As soon as I learned that, I rushed back to help."

"Did Gog create The Nightmare Machine just for us?" Tash asked in a frightened whisper.

The Shi'ido shook his head. "No. I think The Nightmare Machine was his next experiment. But he clearly planned to use you two as his test subjects. That way he could kill two mynocks with one blaster bolt—get his revenge and test his next experiment. But The Nightmare Machine is like all the things we've uncovered. The living planet, the zombies, the virus, and now The Nightmare Machine—they're all just small parts of a much larger plot."

"Project Starscream," Zak said ominously. "Uncle Hoole, I've got so many questions. Where did you go to get this information? And how long have you known Gog?"

"And," Tash added, remembering the file Forceflow

128

had sent them, "what happened during the missing years of your life?"

Hoole frowned. "We are still in too much danger to answer those questions."

Tash cocked her head. "But, Uncle Hoole, you just saved us."

The Shi'ido shook his head sternly. "You saved yourselves from The Nightmare Machine. But none of us are out of danger, I'm afraid."

Zak blinked. "Why? We escaped, didn't we?"

Hoole checked the shuttle's instruments as it swerved off course and blasted away from Hologram Fun World. "For the moment. But Gog is extremely vengeful. I believe that our peril has just begun."

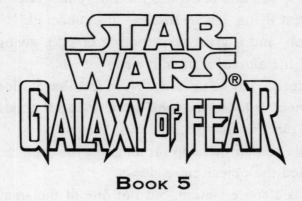
"We're doomed!" Deevee screeched.

Hoole kept calm. Pulling hard on the ship's controls, he veered left. The *Shroud*'s hull groaned under the strain, and they heard the sound of rivets snapping in the metal walls. Despite Hoole's efforts, for a few moments it looked like Deevee had been right. The ship was too close to the side of the massive structure.

"We're not going to make it!" Deevee moaned, covering his photoreceptors with his silver hands.

The *Shroud* scraped along the side of the barrier; the shriek of metal on metal sent shivers down Tash's spine. But then the starship curved up and away from the dark wall and back into the safety of space.

"Great flying, Uncle Hoole!" Tash cheered.

"Yeah, and a great ship too," Zak said, giving the hull of the *Shroud* a friendly pat.

"Indeed," Hoole agreed. "Now, let's have a look at this object. It looks very old, but it does not appear on any of the star charts."

Hoole turned the ship around and this time he approached the object more slowly.

It was a space station, but not one of the small orbital platforms that circled most planets. This looked like the largest space station ever built. If some brilliant beings had wanted to build an artificial continent, or even a small planet, they could not have done better than this.

By the decayed look of the metal, and the pockmarks left by years of asteroid collisions, the station must have been hundreds, maybe thousands of years old. Different areas of the station seemed to have been designed by different engineers as well. It looked as though it had been added to and expanded over the centuries. The station was a dozen kilometers high and its length was impossible to guess—it stretched on forever in every direction.

And it was absolutely dark. Not a single running

light, or landing beacon, or environmental glow panel burned anywhere along its length.

"By the Maker," Deevee said softly. "That is Nespis 8."

"Nespis 8?" Zak asked. "You know this place, Deevee?"

"Only from my extensive historical files," Deevee replied sarcastically. "After all, I was a cultural research droid before I became your caretaker, and I was considered reasonably efficient at my job."

Uncle Hoole seemed unconvinced. "Deevee, I thought Nespis 8 was just a legend. Recheck your memory banks."

"What's Nespis 8?" Tash asked.

The droid paused while his computer brain verified the information. "It is confirmed, Master Hoole. Based on its size, and its apparent age, that is indeed Nespis 8."

"What's Nespis 8?" Tash repeated in exasperation.

Deevee ignored her tone. "According to legend, the Jedi Knights built the space station Nespis 8 as a meeting place for scientists from across the galaxy. The station was devoted to knowledge and learning, and it was considered neutral territory. Even if two planets were involved in a brutal war, their scientists could come to Nespis 8 to do research. As knowledge grew, so did the station, until it was supposed to have grown to the size of a small planet. The legends say that Nespis 8 contained all the knowledge in the galaxy. Including," Deevee added, casting a meaningful look in Tash's direction, "all the wisdom of the Jedi."

"The Jedi," Tash breathed the word as if it were a wish.

"That's correct," the droid affirmed. "It is said that the Jedi maintained a library on Nespis that contained all the writings of their ancient masters. But few dared to look for it. I have heard it said that the halls of Nespis 8 are haunted by the ghost of a Dark Jedi—"

"A *Dark* Jedi?" Zak asked, half-joking. "Now there are dark Jedi too?"

"Dark Jedi," Deevee explained, "were Jedi Knights who served the dark side of the Force. Now please let me finish." The droid paused. "They say Nespis 8 fell to the dark side, and the library was put under a curse forbidding anyone to enter. Only a true Jedi could enter the library and resist the dark-side curse. Of course, all of this is just a legend, and not a very convincing one, in my opinion."

"Whooo!" Zak gave a mock shudder. "Dark Jedi curses—scary stuff."

Hoole dismissed the story with a shrug. "The galaxy

is full of rumors. This one is nothing more than an old spacer's story."

"Even if it's not," Zak said, "it shouldn't bother Tash. Since she's our resident Jedi, she should be safe as a Wookiee in a tree!"

"Shut up, Zak!" Tash snapped. She hadn't meant to react so sharply, but she didn't like Zak joking about her interest in the Jedi. Sometimes she felt strange sensations, almost like warnings—warnings she hoped were the beginning of the Force growing in her. But her dreams of becoming a Jedi Knight had seemed to fall apart recently. On their last adventure, Tash had had the chance to wield a Jedi lightsaber. She had failed miserably. "Besides," Tash grumbled finally, "everyone knows there's no such thing as ghosts."

"Enough," Hoole said. "We have far more urgent concerns. This is where Forceflow told us to meet him, but this station is enormous. I have no idea where we might find—"

The Shi'ido was interrupted by the bleep on an indicator light.

Zak checked the reading, then pointed toward a wide opening in the side of the space station. "Someone just activated a homing beacon. It's coming from that landing bay."

Hoole looked sidelong at his niece. "Well, Tash, it

appears your friend Forceflow is extending his hand to welcome us."

The *Shroud* banked toward the darkened landing bay and settled into a cavernous chamber. To everyone's surprise, as soon as the ship came to a halt, an energy field activated at the edge of the landing bay, blocking out the freezing cold of space. Seconds later, breathable air began to flood the space dock.

"Someone is definitely expecting us," Zak muttered.

"Of course," Tash said. "Forceflow wouldn't let us down."

"Opening the hatch," Hoole declared.

The *Shroud's* hatch opened with a loud squeal that reverberated through the docking bay. Only the dim glow of the ship's landing lights cut through the darkness. As Tash passed in front of one of those lights, she cast a long, thin shadow that stretched out for thirty meters across the floor. Her footsteps echoed mournfully. She stopped. As the echoes died, she thought she heard something else. It sounded like cloth brushing against the skin, or a soft breath . . .

"Hello?" she called out.

"Hello? Hello? Hello?" the walls of the empty space station replied.

"Creepy," Zak whispered. "It doesn't look like there's any one here."

"I suppose the systems could have been automated," Deevee suggested.

Zak looked at his sister, who was staring off into the darkness. "Tash do you sense anything?"

She shrugged. "I don't know. It doesn't matter. I'm not a Jedi, anyway."

Uncle Hoole considered. "Perhaps we should have a look around. Stay close . . ."

Tash wasn't listening. Despite what she had said, she *did* feel something. She just couldn't tell what. In the past, when she sensed danger, it was like a pit opening in her stomach. But this was . . . different. It was like someone was out there, in the darkness, staring at her. She felt like the Ranat in Jabba the Hutt's palace—blind and deaf, trying to touch someone she couldn't see or hear. Before she knew it, she had wandered away from the others, deep into the darkness of the space station. The ship's lights were now only a distant gray blur, almost lost in the thick blackness. Tash waved her hand before her face, but couldn't see it.

She still felt someone's presence.

She groped blindly forward, afraid of stumbling over anything in the dark. She was sure at any moment that she would find something. Something was there, she was sure.

Her hand touched cold metal. She had reached the wall of the docking bay. She felt around for a moment—nothing there. It was just a wall. Confused and frustrated, Tash turned to head back to the others.

As she did, she felt a cold breath on her back. and a heavy hand fell on her shoulder.

ABOUT THE AUTHOR

John Whitman has written several interactive adventures for *Where in the World Is Carmen Sandiego?*, as well as many Star Wars stories for audio and print. He is an executive editor for Time Warner AudioBooks, and lives in Los Angeles, California.